Doubleday Signal Books

SIOUX
SECRET
The Story of
Peary
NUS KID
Olympic Queen
FOR SANDY
RE
RED BELT
THE COAST GUARD
NDUP
BALL, NURSE'S AIDE
FURY
SAILOR
DREAMDUST
THE AIR FORCE
REACH
TS FOR JEAN
SPARK PLUG
TEEN
G ON ICE
THUNDER
RTH, DRUM MAJORETTE
ACK DANGER
RE IN ALASKA
TO THE TOP
FLEET BOY
ADE, FIGHTER FOR
RTY
YSTERY OF HIDDEN
BOR

SCANLON OF THE SUB SERVICE
A SUMMER TO REMEMBER
NAT DUNLAP, JUNIOR "MEDIC"
BLAST-OFF! A Teen Rocket
    Adventure
TWO GIRLS IN NEW YORK
THE MYSTERY OF THE FLOODED
    MINE
CATHY AND LISETTE
EVANS OF THE ARMY
HIGH SCHOOL DROP OUT
DOUBLE TROUBLE
PRO FOOTBALL ROOKIE
THE MYSTERY OF BLUE STAR
    LODGE
ADVENTURE IN DEEPMORE CAVE
FAST BALL PITCHER
HI PACKETT, JUMPING CENTER
NURSE IN TRAINING
SHY GIRL: The Story of Eleanor
    Roosevelt
SKI PATROL
BIG BAND
GINNY HARRIS ON STAGE
GRACIE
THREE CHEERS FOR POLLY
TV DANCER
SECOND YEAR NURSE
ARTHUR ASHE: Tennis Champion
FEAR RIDES HIGH

GINNY HARR

GINNY HARRIS ON STAGE

By Evelyn Fiore

ILLUSTRATED BY
ANNA MARIE MAGAGNA

Doubleday & Company, Inc.
Garden City, New York

F
Fio

Library of Congress Catalog Card Number 65–18295

Copyright © 1965 by Doubleday & Company, Inc.

All Rights Reserved

Printed in the United States of America

Prepared by **R** Rutledge Books

CONTENTS

CHAPTER 1

Bad Beginning

Ginny Harris stopped outside her World History room, held her breath, and counted slowly to ten. The bell rang and the last students hurried past her into the room. Still, Ginny held her breath and hoped. Miss Cameron, the Drama Club coach, had said that this trick of holding one's breath was the way many famous actors cured their last-minute stage fright. It ought to work for a girl who was just plain nervous!

"The bell rang, stupid!" It was Emmy Price, her best friend, talking to her. "What are you waiting for?"

Ginny let out her breath. No use. She was still so nervous that she was afraid to shake her head for fear her bones would grind together. "I can't go in," she whispered. "I just can't. I have to give that report today!"

"But you are prepared," Emmy said, shaking Ginny's arm. "We went to the library together, remember? You know everything about Greece! Come on, Ginny—oops, here comes Elgar!"

Emmy let go of Ginny's sleeve and ducked into the room as Mr. Elgar, the World History teacher, walked over to close the door.

"Ginny? Are you with us today, or have you had a better offer?" Mr. Elgar was smiling. He was known around Glenside High as a great man with a joke. Ginny knew he didn't mean to annoy her. He kidded everybody. But the students seated near the door had heard him, and their laughs brought heat to Ginny's cheeks as she edged down to her seat at the back of the room. What a way to start the day—a report to give in her first class, and every eye turned upon her even before she was in the room!

The eyes were already turned away, for Mr. Elgar was the kind of teacher who got his students' full attention— or else. But Ginny, sitting low in her seat, felt that her class mates were still laughing. She took some more deep breaths. Finally she was able to take her eyes from her desk and look up.

It was all completely crazy. Ginny knew that. She was a quiet, reliable student, and Mr. Elgar's remark did not mean that he suspected her of planning to cut class. She knew that the others had laughed more to flatter him than because they thought Ginny was a girl to laugh at.

Ginny Harris was shy. Not just quiet. She was so shy it hurt. Her sister Madeline always said there ought to be another word for how shy Ginny was. Even at the family dinner table she had trouble getting out an answer if somebody said to her, "What's new?" In class, her throat went dry when she was called on to answer an ordinary question. And on terrible days like this one, when she had a report to give . . .

Mr. Elgar's voice cut through Ginny's thoughts. "Slow down, Cappy. The train will wait." At the front of the room, Cappy Roberts nodded and went on, more slowly, with his report. Ginny hadn't even known he had been called on. She made herself pay attention.

"And please stand up!" Mr. Elgar told Cappy.

Cappy snapped to attention, gave Mr. Elgar a mock salute, and went on.

Ginny was torn with envy. That was the way to be. When Mr. Elgar kidded Cappy, he didn't come apart at the seams!

"And now, for the report on Greece . . . oh, yes, Ginny Harris." The words came like blows. Ginny couldn't breathe. Going slowly to the front, she caught Emmy's eye and tried to smile. As she swallowed and began to speak, she couldn't hear herself.

She had hoped so hard that this time it would be different! But her hands were damp, as they always were. It was just as difficult to make the words come out. She remembered that Mr. Elgar always told students to look at the audience—first one person, then another. You held their attention that way. Ginny, as she talked, looked at Emmy, then at Cappy. She was so busy talking and looking that she lost her place among the cards on which she had put her notes.

This was bad. It was awful. There was dead silence while she spread the cards on Mr. Elgar's desk and tried to find her place. "Ginny?" Mr. Elgar called to her. She threw him a wild look. Where was it—exports, trade— where *was* it?

"If this is between the acts, bring on the soft drinks!" came the voice from the front row. It was Jim Howe, who could be counted on to needle when he got a chance. Nobody laughed, and Mr. Elgar told Jim sharply that if he had any more comments to make he could make them in the principal's office. But for Ginny it was the end. She found her place and began again, but her shaking voice could not be heard. From the back rows came calls of "Louder . . . Can't hear."

Ginny's trembling fingers searched for the next card, and suddenly all her cards were on the floor. Bending to pick them up, she thought in despair, "I will never get up again. I will never be able to face them."

And then the bell rang.

Ginny stooped over the cards until she saw the last pair of feet go out. Only then did she straighten up.

"Good report, Ginny," Mr. Elgar said, writing in his record book. "Let's hear the rest of it tomorrow."

"Oh, no!" Ginny burst out in a wail. "Oh please, Mr. Elgar—I can't go through it again!"

Mr. Elgar looked at her thoughtfully. "All right, calm down. You can hand it in written. But you ought to try. Until Howe bothered you, you were doing very well."

Ginny's heart soared. She could hand it in written! "I will write a thousand pages!" she told herself in a burst of gratitude toward Mr. Elgar, as she collected her books and headed down the hall. "I will hand in the best report on Greece he has ever had!"

And the report would probably be excellent, too. Long ago, Ginny had realized that she had to make up in her written work and on tests for the poor way she always performed in class work. Her written reports always got A's, and her tests seldom fell below 90. She could do anything—as long as she didn't have to do it out loud!

Ginny sailed toward the stairs, light-hearted with relief. The worst part of the day was already behind her, and it was only second period! Now, if she hurried, she would have a full 45 minutes—her whole study period—down in the Drama Club work room, hammering nails and painting away on the sets for the play they were preparing. And if she was really lucky, there would be nobody down there to bother her at all!

She wasn't that lucky. Ginny was on the Sets and Props Committee, and when she opened the door of the basement work room the noise sounded as if the other members were all there too.

"Ginny!" Roz Blaine called. "Hurry up—I've been waiting for you. We have to get this flat finished."

There really wasn't much to it. The Drama Club's Set Design Committee, under Miss Cameron's direction, had drawn careful designs for the setting of each scene in *As You Like It*, the Shakespeare play that had been chosen for performance. These small drawings had to be transferred, in much larger size, of course, to the "flats"—nine-foot-high wooden frames covered with canvas which would be painted to become the actual backgrounds on the stage. "The Forest of Arden," finished, stood drying against the far wall of the work room. Now it was time to do "The Duke's Palace."

Miss Cameron and the art teacher, who was helping her, had carefully taught the committee how to square off the small drawings, then block off the large "flat" into the same number of squares—much larger ones, naturally. Then they copied what was in each small square on to the matching square of the flat, drawing each bit much larger.

When Ginny had first joined the Drama Club, at the beginning of the year, she had never expected to do more than help with rough work—she liked to hammer and saw things and she could sew very well. But she had found that she was fairly good also at the actual painting of scenes. And it was she who had learned to make the neatest "snap-lines," a much quicker way of marking off the flats into the squares than to draw each line by itself.

"You have good hands," Roz said now, as she watched Ginny tack a piece of string to the top of the flat, rub the string heavily with black chalk, and tack it tightly to the bottom end. Then she simply snapped the string against the canvas, and there was a straight, thin black line. "It's fun," Ginny told Roz.

Everything about the Drama Club was more fun than Ginny had had since she had been in Glenside High. As Roz and the others drifted off, leaving her to mark out the flat alone, she thought about how close she had come to not joining the club. Last year, when she was a junior, she had joined the Girls' Chorus and the Camera Club —just to keep her mother from always reminding her of her older sister Madeline's many activities.

At the start of her senior year she had asked for no activities at all. She had been surprised when Mr. Feld, who advised students, had told her he wanted her to go out for the Drama Club. "I know you will say no," Mr. Feld had said, the day he called her in for a conference, "so I'm not asking—I'm telling you."

"Me—in the Drama Club?" Ginny had gasped. "On the *stage?*"

"All right, not on the stage," Mr. Feld had said. "I'm not asking for miracles. Miss Cameron needs all kinds of help for that group—carpenters, painters, people who can sew. You can't imagine how many committees there are behind each show."

"I do like to make things. And I like to sew." Ginny

had given him her attention then. Mr. Feld was too smart to come right out with it, but Ginny knew perfectly well that this was the kind of thing people made you do "for your own good"—and for once in her life she decided to go along with it. A week later, she had gone to her first meeting, and had been swept away by Miss Cameron's energy, charm, and the excitement of planning all the sets for *As You Like It*.

And the best thing about it, Ginny thought as she rubbed the last black snap-line, was just what was going on now—there was so much to do, always, that you could be busy all the time. If you didn't want to sit around talking, you didn't have to.

"Ah, my Juliet!" said a boy's voice behind her. Surprised, Ginny pulled the line so hard it broke off. She turned to see Cappy Roberts and Mike Dyne, the boy who had the male lead, "Orlando," in *As You Like It*. It was Mike who had spoken, and he looked as surprised as she did.

"I'm sorry—I thought you were Helena," he said. "Gosh, I know Miss Cameron's always saying how much alike you two look, but I never realized it before."

"Especially from the back," Cappy added. Ginny smiled slowly. Helena Lang, who played the female lead, "Rosalind," was a tall, thin girl, with blonde hair that fell straight to her shoulders, and dark eyes set wide apart in a pale face—a description which, Ginny knew, fit her too, if you looked fast. In fact, she and Helena were so nearly

15

the same size and shape that often Miss Cameron got Ginny to try on costumes if Helena wasn't around. But there were so many important differences! Helena's brown eyes were lively, eager—they didn't have the sad look that Ginny saw too often in her mirror. Helena had confidence, charm . . . friends.

"Let me help you with that," Mike said, throwing down his books and kneeling beside Ginny. "Fair's fair—it's my fault it broke."

"You don't have to," Ginny said. "I mean it's not hard —I can do it. Besides, you aren't on the committee."

Mike sat back on his heels, grinning. He had a nice smile, but it was his deep, attractive voice rather than his looks that had won him the Orlando part. "You mean I haven't got a union card? Or are the actors too low class to mix with the artists?"

Ginny smiled back and accepted his help in silence. Actually, she had meant the opposite—actors were too *high* class to be down here crawling around. She knew it was silly, but when she watched play practice she couldn't get over feeling that anyone who could stand up there on the stage and act must be made of a different kind of flesh and blood from hers.

Cappy had joined the others at the far end of the work room, and the sound of talk and laughter made Ginny very much aware of the quiet between her and Mike as they stretched and snapped the line. Finally she swallowed and asked, "If you thought I was Helena, why did you say 'Juliet'? She's Rosalind in the play."

Mike's face grew red. "Well—it's kind of a dumb private joke. It's like we figure the most famous play Shakespeare wrote was 'Romeo and Juliet,' and—they're the most famous couple in the world—and in this play Helena and I are the lovers, I mean the ones that are paired off . . ." Ginny had gone red, too, as Mike stumbled over the word "lovers." She wished she had never asked. Any other girl would laugh and say, "Well, *Romeo!* Imagine my not recognizing you!" Or something. But she couldn't. Dumb, clumsy, she only nodded and went on working. Helena would have said . . .

Oh, what did it matter what Helena would have said? She wasn't Helena. She wasn't any girl with an easy word for friends. She wasn't a girl who could join in and be part of things. Evidently her feeling rubbed off on Mike, because he couldn't find anything else to say, either.

"Five minutes ago I was happy," Ginny thought. "What *is* it with me? As long as I'm working, I'm fine. I even talked to Roz and kidded around with her—about what we were doing. The minute somebody comes along and makes it more personal—like Mike—I'm struck dumb. What's the matter with me, anyway?"

Miss Cameron's voice suddenly rang through the work room. "Ginny Harris! I need Ginny right away."

CHAPTER 2

How Do You Get
to Be Somebody Else?

Before Ginny could answer, Miss Cameron's tall, spare figure appeared from behind the lockers. "There you are! I've been looking everywhere! Nobody in the whole school knew where you were!"

"Oh, nobody ever bothers about where I am," Ginny might have answered, except that Miss Cameron didn't want an answer. She never did. She had too much to say herself, and too little time in which to say it.

"Listen, Helena's got a test or something in fourth period, and it's the only time Mrs. Ricket can fit that costume on her for the second act. She will have to fit it on you instead."

Ginny nodded. Mrs. Ricket, the teacher who was making most of the costumes for the show, had become used to fitting Helena's outfits on her. "I have fourth-period lunch," she told Miss Cameron. "I will get up to Mrs. Ricket's room about half through the period, if that's all right."

"Fine," Miss Cameron said. She raised her voice. "Say —you kids over in the corner, is this a working committee or a senior social?"

Mike Dyne, making his voice also loud enough to be heard across the room, answered, "Miss Cameron, since you ask, I feel it my duty to tell you—" He was cut short by Cappy's sneaker, which came flying through the air and landed with perfect aim right in Mike's middle. Miss Cameron bellowed, "Cappy! Can't you at least wait until I'm out of the room? You might have hit *me!*"

"Not a chance, Miss Cameron," Cappy replied with a big grin. "I can't do much, but I can send a ball where I want it to go!"

Everybody but Ginny laughed and yelled, "But that was a *sneaker!*" Even Miss Cameron was laughing, her brief moment of anger drowned in the general good humor. In the midst of it all, the bell rang. Ginny gave her hands a quick wash and escaped.

When the fourth period arrived, she ate her ham sandwich quickly in a corner of the lunch room, and took her milk with her to Mrs. Ricket's room. Mrs. Ricket would yell bloody murder if Ginny were a minute late, although she wouldn't be ready herself.

Ginny had time to finish her milk and eat half a

chocolate bar before Mrs. Ricket came in. "Keep doing that and we will have to let out the costumes," Mrs. Ricket said, with a long look at the chocolate.

Ginny laughed. "You should talk to my mother, Mrs. Ricket. She keeps trying to make me gain weight and you keep telling me I had better not. Anyway—it's Helena the costumes have to fit, not me."

"Helena Lang is a nice girl, but I would just as soon it was you and not she," Mrs. Ricket said, helping Ginny into the tights and green velvet blouse in which Rosalind pretended she was a boy in the second act of *As You Like It*. "At least you are always where I can get my hands on you. That other one—she's in so many clubs, I don't know how she ever found time to try out for this part."

"But she's so good!" Ginny protested. She held still while Mrs. Ricket placed the long black page-boy wig over her blonde hair, and on top of it the green velvet cap. Narrowing her eyes, Ginny looked at herself in the full-length mirror. She did look like Helena—she looked exactly the way Helena looked in the costume, anyway. Funny, how two girls could look so much alike—and yet let anyone try to put her up on that stage in Helena's place, even for two minutes—what a difference there would be!

"Hold still," Mrs. Ricket muttered, her mouth full of pins. "I have to take up this seam a bit." Sun poured in on Ginny, making her sleepy. From the ball field three stories below, voices came thinly up to the little room. She thought of Cappy throwing the sneaker, and laughed suddenly, so that Mrs. Ricket stuck her with a pin.

"We had better get you out of this. It's late," Mrs. Ricket said. "Good heavens, I've sewed you up the side! Just a minute, I will have to rip it out."

The first bell rang just as Ginny finished buttoning on her own blouse, and she grabbed up her books and ran for the fourth floor. She threw herself into her seat a split second before the last bell rang.

At first Ginny thought people were looking around at her and smiling because of her quick dash. Then she told herself crossly that it was just like World History all over again—she was imagining it.

"Nobody is looking at me!" she thought firmly, staring straight into Jim Howe's eyes as he turned around and grinned at her. Ginny ran a nervous hand down the buttons of her blouse. They were all fastened. She felt the side of her skirt. That was all right, too.

Several other people turned around, some looking surprised, some smiling. Ginny's cheeks grew warm. What could it be? There was nothing wrong with her shoes. She didn't have on two different ones. Maybe her face was dirty?

Ginny fished a mirror out of her purse. Stealing a look into it, she gasped. In the mirror, she could see why everyone was smiling. The page-boy wig! Golly—she was still wearing it! It hadn't come off when Mrs. Ricket pulled off the hat, and she had moved so fast neither of them had realized!

Ginny looked up and met the eyes of the girl who sat next to her—a girl named Merry Hall, who was on the Wardrobe Committee of the Drama Club. Merry was smiling. Wouldn't anybody look twice when a girl who had been a blonde all her life turned up in class with long black hair?

Ginny scribbled a note, tore it out of her notebook and passed it to Merry. "I haven't dyed my hair," she had written. "This is the wig from the Rosalind costume —I forgot I had it on. Maybe it's my chance to find out if *brunettes* have more fun."

Merry glanced at it, grinned, and passed it to the boy next to her. In a few minutes, the whole class knew why Ginny was wearing a black wig.

For the first time in her life, Ginny was the center of attention—and didn't want to go somewhere and die because of it. She didn't even bother taking off the wig until the end of the period, when she carried it back to Mrs. Ricket's room.

All day long Ginny remembered how she had felt in the wig—like somebody else. Somebody who could laugh at herself and write a funny note about it. Somebody who didn't at all mind being looked at.

Thinking about the wig should have made that Friday night at home easier. It didn't seem to help much. Ginny didn't care for Friday nights. Her sister Madeline and husband Jack were always there for dinner. And Madeline meant questions. Tonight it was questions about summer jobs.

"You mean you haven't looked at all?" Madeline said. "But Ginny—all the good ones will be snapped up by now! Why don't you go down and see—"

"Maybe Ginny has some ideas of her own," Jack interrupted mildly.

"Well . . ." Ginny began. She hadn't really given it much thought. She sighed. Madeline was right—she would have to look. Crossing her fingers, Ginny said, "As a matter of fact, I made an appointment for next week with the office at school that helps find jobs.

They will have some ideas and send me on interviews."

It wasn't true, but she could make the appointment on Monday—and for now it had stopped Madeline. "Do you mind if I hurry?" she added, as she got up to bring in the coffee. "Emmy's expecting me."

Madeline looked up quickly. "Are you two going over to that new teen-age club they have at the Y—whatever they call it?"

"The Pumpkin Room," Ginny said. "No—we're not going there tonight." She managed to escape before she had to confess that she had never been there.

The Pumpkin Room was, she knew, a teen "night club," modeled on several others around the country, where members could sit at tables covered with cloths, order sandwiches and soft drinks, and listen to the kind of music they liked.

"Live Bands!" announced the posters outside the Y. Or sometimes, "Live Entertainment Straight from Greenwich Village, New York!" Ginny turned hot and cold when she had to go past the Y to get to Emmy's house. Always there were boys hanging about on the steps, waiting for their dates. Ginny felt sure they were just waiting for her to somehow make a fool of herself, like stubbing her toe.

Tonight, she was lucky. When she started out, it began to sprinkle. By the time she got to the Y, the last boy had turned his back on the street and gone inside. Ginny could hear the "live band" all the way down the block. The music followed her way down to the corner as she waited for the lights to change. It sent a strange tingle through her toes.

She pulled a scarf from her pocket and tied it around her head, but the sound still came through. A wild thought swept into her mind as she started to cross the street: there wasn't a single reason why *she* couldn't go to The Pumpkin Room. Most people went stag, unless they were going steady.

Ginny's heart thumped. She hesitated in the middle of Main Street and half turned. A car horn honked loudly in her ears, and she leaped forward as a furious driver swept by, yelling "Dope!"

Ginny fell against the curb, skinned her knee, and ended up leaning against the corner mail box. She felt silly, but she couldn't stop laughing.

Then somebody took her elbow and said, "I'm sorry about that. Are you hurt?" A tall young man was looking down at her with concern.

To Ginny, looking up and up, he seemed ten feet tall, dark, and as strange as though he had just arrived from Mars. He gave her arm a shake and said, "Good grief, are you crying? Gosh—you did get hurt! Let me see!" He was actually bending to look at her knee when Ginny pushed him away.

"I'm not crying. I'm laughing," she said, and the laughter stopped. "And I'm not hurt." She remembered her manners. "Thank you."

"You are bleeding," the young man pointed out. Blood was indeed dripping down into Ginny's shoe. "You fell pretty hard. I feel terrible—it was crazy of me to yell at you like that."

"You mean it was you in that car?" Ginny glared up at him. "Do you always drive like that?"

The young man grinned. "Sure. I obey the lights, drive in my own lane, never tail-gate, and observe courtesy rules at all times. I even watch out for people who walk out into traffic to do their heavy thinking."

Ginny laughed. She was glad it was dark enough to hide her flush. All at once, she realized she was standing on the corner of Main Street, talking to a total stranger —she, who couldn't think of two words to say to boys she had known since ninth grade! She stopped laughing and bent over to dry her knee with her handkerchief.

"I've got a medicine kit in the car," the young man said. "Let me get you a Band-Aid or something. Or can I drive you wherever you were going?"

"No!" burst from Ginny, as though he had suggested setting fire to the Town Hall. "Of course not! I mean— I'm fine. Don't bother." She edged away, turned and fled around the corner, down Palmer Street, aware of a last glimpse of surprise on the stranger's face.

She could see that look all the way to Emmy's house. Yet somehow, when Emmy eagerly questioned her, she found she didn't want to describe him or talk about him at all. She felt too foolish—running away like that, when he had only been trying to be nice. But certainly she couldn't have accepted a lift from him. "Especially if you've never seen him at school or around town," as Emmy pointed out. "Do you think he works here or is visiting or something?"

"How should I know?" Ginny asked. "He had one of those little cars—red, I think—and of course he wasn't from school. He was much older. I didn't wait around to get his whole life story!"

"Well, it's kind of thrilling," Emmy said. They were out on her porch, Emmy on the swing, Ginny on the top step with her arms wrapped around her knees, watching the soft, light rain come down on the quiet street. Now and then a car full of young people shot past, but the only other sound was the squeak of the swing as Emmy set it moving.

"I sure wish some more excitement would turn up," Emmy said, with a sigh.

Ginny nodded. "Coming over, I suddenly had this crazy idea. I thought maybe I would phone you from the drug store and get you to meet me at The Pumpkin Room."

Emmy sat up straight. "Crazy, nothing! Haven't I been nagging you to go there with me? I turned down a chance to go with Merry and her crowd tonight, if you want to know, just because you were coming over and I knew you would take my head off if I mentioned going."

"Well, you should have said yes," Ginny told her.

"You shouldn't let my problems interfere with your life."

"Next time we will both go," Emmy said. "Ginny, you know you really want to! I mean—tonight proves it, doesn't it? After all, it's just the same kids we go to school with. They don't turn into witches because it's night and they are outside the school!"

"Aren't you forgetting that I'm no ball of fire with them even in school?" Ginny reminded her. "I can't think what to answer if somebody says hello to me. I fall over my own feet coming into the lunch room. I'd be great, sitting at a table at The Pumpkin Room! But listen, Emmy—next week, you go."

"Both of us will go," Emmy insisted. Ginny knew one thing for certain: if she lost her nerve and didn't go next Friday, she would really be alone. Emmy wasn't going to be held back forever. Quite a few invitations had come her way lately. Emmy wasn't a forward type, but sooner or later every normal girl began to gain more confidence about boys and parties and being with people her own age.

"Except me," Ginny thought, as she lay in bed later that night. "If I am making any progress that way, it's so slow it doesn't even show. Like watching a plant grow." Yes—but when you watched a plant grow, you saw nothing until, all of a sudden, there was a flower. Would that ever happen to her?

Ginny sat up suddenly and clasped her knees. What about the way she had stood there on Main Street tonight, laughing and talking with a handsome stranger? What about the way she had laughed off the black wig, when she had found herself wearing it in class?

Maybe if she could forget that she was Ginny Harris, the shy one—maybe then she could start being like everyone else. Only—how did you go about doing it?

CHAPTER 3

The Big Night

"Ginny," Miss Cameron called from the stage, "come up here, will you?"

Ginny pushed over to Emmy the programs she had been folding. The wild note in Miss Cameron's voice didn't mean anything. Everyone had grown used to it as performance day came closer. Now when Miss Cameron merely said good morning it sounded like somebody crying out "Run for your lives!"

Ginny raced down to the stage like a fire horse. It was so marvelous to have somebody call out for you—as if you were absolutely the only one who could do whatever had to be done!

"Here," Miss Cameron said, pulling Ginny to center stage and then pushing her around. "Stand in for Helena, will you, so the boys can test the lighting set-up?"

Light flashed against Ginny's face. Patiently she stood, turned and moved as Miss Cameron ordered. She had done this kind of thing so often that it no longer made her nervous to be on the stage instead of behind it. The fact that she looked like Helena had made Miss Cameron's life much simpler.

By now, Ginny was completely involved in *As You Like It*. She knew how to work the lights and open the new velvet curtain and move the painted back-drop scenes on and off stage. She knew everyone's part almost as well as the actors themselves.

Helena's part, of course, she knew best of all. In her mind, she ran through the scene they were lighting. "The Duke's Palace," she thought. "Here's where the fountain will be. Here's where I turn to talk to Celia." As Coralee Bannon, in her part as "Celia," came up to her, Ginny repeated to herself: "'Alas, what danger will it be to us, Maid as we are, to travel forth so far?'"

"Over here, Ginny," Miss Cameron directed from the orchestra pit below. "Now, Rosalind sits down—"

"No, that's later," Ginny said quickly. "You remember, Miss Cameron—this is where she says, 'Were it not better, because that I am more than common tall, That I did suit me all points like a man!' She can't sit down here—you said we have to see how tall she is."

Miss Cameron flipped through the pages of the play in her mind. "I'm losing my mind," she moaned. "Of course! Ginny, do you know the whole part that well?"

Before Ginny could answer, Emmy's voice came from the back of the room. "She can do it standing on her head, Miss Cameron. Every word and every bit of 'business' you've worked out. Everything!"

Miss Cameron nodded. "Fine, then you are official understudy for Rosalind—I mean Helena. She's the only principal actor who hasn't got one so far. Let's get on, now."

Ginny tried to give Emmy a dirty look, but she was running around taking orders for sandwiches. Oh well, what did it matter? If anything really happened to one of the chief actors, they would simply change the date of the performance.

Mike Dyne and Ralph Pearson went across the street to the drug store and brought back a load of sandwiches and sodas. When Ginny came out front again, her heart sank to see everyone already set up in friendly little groups, eating and talking away. Her eyes sought out Emmy, but there was no hope there, either. Emmy was bounded on all four sides by people, mostly boys.

Bracing herself, Ginny went to get her food, and discovered that the only thing left was an orange soda. No sandwich. Ralph Pearson saw her looking around. "Oh no," he said. "Everybody will think Mike and I pinched the 35 cents and cut one sandwich off the order. Hey!" He held up a hand for attention. "Where's the pig who took two sandwiches? Come on, speak up!"

"Never mind," Ginny whispered in agony. "I don't need it!" She rushed away before Ralph could shout again, and found herself a seat at the end of a row.

Down toward the left, Miss Cameron sat pushing her short, straight hair off her face with one hand and drinking out of a paper cup with the other, talking all the while. Ginny tried to hear. Miss Cameron had interesting stories to tell; some about her cousin Constance Vane, a famous actress in the theater. Ginny shifted a few seats closer to the group around Miss Cameron, and found herself next to Mike Dyne.

He gave her a friendly nod. "How are you doing? Say listen—take this half of my sandwich. I have a couple of candy bars in my pocket." He tapped his shirt.

Ginny quickly handed back the sandwich he shoved at her. "Oh, no, please—you eat it."

Mike grinned and put it back in her lap. "This could go on all night. I insist that you have it. It will make me feel like a real sport."

Inside Ginny a little voice said, "Take it, say thank you, laugh, and eat it up. It's not a bag of gold, it's half of a sandwich. It's just a friendly gesture."

But habit was too strong—the habit of not wanting special notice. "I really don't want it," she said.

Mike's grin faded. He frowned. "All right, if that's how it is."

There was no time for brooding, but that didn't keep Ginny from hating herself. She had done it again. She had wanted to smile, to reach out—to let Mike know that she felt friendly too. What was it, always, that made her close up and run away? Why was it that she could stand up on the stage and practically talk back to Miss Cameron without a worry . . . and yet want to jump up and run because a boy made a friendly sound in her direction?

During the next school days, Ginny felt more and more often as if she were really two people. In a social group she was as quiet as ever. But the moment the kidding around gave place to work, she forgot to think about herself and became lost in the fun of putting a play together.

Then all at once, the big night arrived. Afterward, when the Drama Club members compared notes, not one could remember anything about the entire day. Helena and Ralph Pearson were the only ones who would admit that they had eaten dinner. "I'm a growing girl," Helena excused herself. "I need to keep up my strength. But boy— if you think we are nervous, you ought to see my folks. My dad had to lie down when he came home from work, he's so worn out from *my* stage fright!"

Ginny, who was pressing the purple gown Helena would wear in the first act, smiled to herself. What would have happened at her house, she wondered, if she were facing Helena's job instead of the things back stage she would be doing? If she had been the one to go out there, her mother and father would have had to tie her down to keep her from taking the first bus out of town. Her folks didn't know how lucky they were. They were coming, of course. Everyone was coming. There was even talk that Miss Cameron's famous actress cousin was coming from New York.

Time raced on. Miss Cameron, in a shabby old smock over a smart black dress, was everywhere at once.

By 7:30, everyone was in costume for the opening scenes. Orchestra members were tramping about in the pit, setting out instruments and music. Everybody was too worn out to be scared any more. A kind of strange calm settled down. Mike Dyne looked up at Ginny when she brought him his wig.

"Hey, Ginny, is this sword hanging right?"

Ginny fixed the sword, helped Coralee with her costume, and then ran down to Helena's part of the dressing room to answer a cry of dismay. Helena had eaten so well she had burst a hook getting into the purple gown. Quickly, Ginny sewed it back on.

Emmy, with the others who were to take tickets and show people to their seats, had long disappeared out front. The audience was coming in, finding seats. The orchestra gave out a few trial notes. Mike and the other boys in the first scene stood waiting in the wings, Miss Cameron watching them nervously.

The orchestra grew silent. Up in the control room, Jim and Ralph began dimming the lights. There were two raps from the bow of Mr. Channing, the orchestra leader, and the music began. Ginny stole up behind Miss

Cameron as the curtain swept apart and Orlando came on stage and waited, as he had been directed, for the clapping to die down before he began to speak.

Standing with Miss Cameron, Ginny could feel herself growing calm as the play got under way. Everything went perfectly. Nobody forgot a line. Nobody's costume split, nobody dropped anything. Helena and Coralee looked beautiful and spoke well. Miss Cameron's back grew less stiff. She muttered to herself, "This can't go on!" as the first act drew to a close.

Just as the curtain closed and the orchestra struck up its between-acts music, Ed Paley pushed past Ginny and spoke in low tones to Miss Cameron. She clapped her hand to her forehead, stared at him and, without a word, turned and hurried toward the dressing room. Ginny had the queer feeling that she had gone deaf. Everything seemed to be happening in slow motion and utter silence. As she headed for the dressing room, she crashed into a wild-eyed Emmy, who grabbed her and gasped, "Have you heard?"

"What? What?" Ginny demanded. Was it a fire? She sniffed. There was no smoke, no shouting.

"Helena's father just had a heart attack."

Emmy vanished in the direction of the back-stage peep hole, where a shifting group of students was trying to peer into the audience without being seen.

Ginny's first thought was, "Poor Helena!" Suddenly the whole back-stage area was choked with alarmed students hurrying this way and that. She tried to push toward the girls' dressing room, but was stopped by Mike Dyne. "What's going on, will somebody please tell me? Helena's in there ripping off her second-act clothes, and Miss Cameron's about to burst—"

Ginny told him, and added, "Somebody better tell Mr. Channing to keep the music going."

The people blocking her moved suddenly and she almost fell into the dressing room, as Miss Cameron pulled open the door and stuck out a white, desperate face. Beyond her, Ginny saw Helena buttoning on a shirt, and heard Coralee saying, "But, Helena, what about the play? What about the show? You can't just—"

"Wrong," Helena said briefly, bending down to tie her shoes. "My dad's being taken to the hospital and that's where I'm going." She came out, stopping only to say, "I'm sorry, Miss Cameron, but I have to."

"Do you want someone to go with you?" Miss Cameron called, but Helena called back, "Thanks, my brother's waiting outside," and disappeared.

Miss Cameron pushed Ginny into the dressing room. "Fast," she said. "Into the second-act costume. Celia—Coralee—help her." She snapped her fingers to indicate what she wanted, and before Ginny had caught her breath they had put her into the tights and blouse in which Rosalind acted as Ganymede in the second act of *As You Like It*.

"Thank heaven you won't be on till scene four," Miss Cameron muttered, pulling on over Ginny's hair the black page-boy wig, and settling the feathered cap that completed the outfit. Without thinking, Ginny felt for the short sword at her side and Miss Cameron said, "That's it! Just remember to walk around like a gallant young chap—and we are all set. You can catch your breath now."

Dimly, Ginny realized that the orchestra was no longer filling in time out front. She had no idea when the second act had started, but now she heard voices: Orlando was talking to his servant, Adam, played by Phil Baynes. Act Two, Scene Three, clicked her mind. She stared at Miss Cameron.

"Take it easy, girl, you can do it." Miss Cameron put

an arm around Ginny's shoulders. "You know the part backward."

"Me!" Ginny gasped. Until that second she had not actually taken in what was going on. She tried to pull away, but Miss Cameron's arm was an iron band urging her straight toward the wings. "Me? You don't know what you are saying! I can't go out there! Miss Cameron, I will *die!* In front of all those—oh, no! I will dry up, you don't know what happens to me when people—"

"I do know. *It's not going to happen now.* The minute you get out there you'll *be Rosalind.* You'll be fine."

Like a frightened horse, Ginny tried to pull away. Miss Cameron faced her around and stared into her eyes. "Listen, Ginny—you've got to. Either you do it, or everything we've worked on so hard falls down on our heads."

As the boys came off the stage, Mike Dyne caught Ginny's hand in a tight grip. "Get going, pal," he said. Somebody else gave her a shove. The next minute Ginny Harris, who was afraid to answer "present" to her name in class, stood out on the stage in front of 800 people.

CHAPTER 4

It Doesn't Matter
What You Look Like

Ginny's next really conscious moment was when she stood holding Mike's hand on one side, Coralee's on the other, and was bowing and smiling, bowing and smiling.

It was over! The final lines had been spoken, the curtain was down, and now the audience was clapping loud and long. Two by two the other actors left the stage, and she and Mike stepped forward to take a bow alone.

"This is me?" Ginny thought, as she turned toward Mike and bowed the way Miss Cameron had told her to do. "Medal of Honor," Mike was saying under his breath. "Purple Heart. Valor above and beyond. You were great!"

Coming off stage, Ginny heard the same thing from everyone. Miss Cameron hugged her fiercely and said, "Ginny! I told you you could do it!"

Ginny nodded, not able to speak. Had she done it? She must have. There had been clapping, and now everybody was pushing around, patting her on the back. Somehow she had acted through the whole of Helena's part! She hadn't died out there on stage. She hadn't missed a line, lost her voice, forgotten anything! Letting herself be led toward the dressing room, Ginny began to come back to earth.

Suddenly Ginny sat up and stared at herself in the mirror. Out there in front of those people, she hadn't been Ginny Harris! She had been "Rosalind." She had been "Rosalind" so completely that she still couldn't remember anything she had said or done.

". . . unless you want to call your mother," Emmy's voice came thinly through to her. "Or we can stop over at your house and you can get into a dress. We won't be too late."

Ginny realized that the dressing room was full of chatter. Roz Blaine put her dark head around the curtain that separated Helena's "dressing room" from Coralee's and shouted, "You were wonderful, Ginny! How did you ever know the part like that!" Smiling her thanks, Ginny thought, "Yesterday you didn't even know my name for sure. Isn't fame wonderful!"

"You haven't answered me," Emmy said. "Come down to earth. Do you want to go to the party in your jeans or do you want to change?"

Ginny answered, "You know I'm not going to the

party." They had been fighting about the party ever since Miss Cameron had announced that she was giving one. Every time Emmy had brought it up, Ginny's answer had been the same. "You go if you want to, but I'm not!"

"You have to come to the party," Emmy urged. "It's all different now. Don't you *feel* different?"

Ginny considered. She did feel different. Her heart was beating hard, her face was pink with excitement. Suddenly she said, "All right. Come home while I change."

"That's my girl!" Emmy exclaimed. They pushed their way out of the building, through a yard filled with excited students, and cut across the ball field.

"Wear your green silk," Emmy decided. "That's not too dress-up for a party where the great Constance Vane is going to be present!"

Ginny's house was dark when they got there. Emmy scribbled a note for Ginny's parents while Ginny ran up and changed. Ginny brushed her hair until it shone and found a small green bow to clip low on one side. She even put on lipstick with a brush Madeline had once given her. Then she and Emmy walked down to Main Street and caught the bus to Miss Cameron's place.

It looked like a party even before they got to the door. Cars, bicycles and Cappy Roberts' red Vespa made a tight parking line the whole length of the block. Noise came out to meet them. Finally, when nobody opened the door, Emmy turned the knob and they walked in.

The small living room, kitchen, and bedroom had not

been designed to hold 35 young people, plus four or five teachers who had come to join the party. They were packed in, as Emmy said, like olives in a jar. At first Ginny had that familiar turn-and-run feeling. There was so much noise and laughter, music and confusion! But Emmy was behind her, one hand firmly pushing Ginny forward.

Everybody greeted Ginny, but nobody made her feel as though she stood out. Mike Dyne stuck a glass in her hand and said, "Let's see you push *that* back in my face!"

So far so good. Emmy had left her, but she didn't feel scared. Not a bit. She looked around and thought, "Golly —I'm glad I came!"

"Hey, Ginny. How did it feel, up there?" Cappy Roberts appeared suddenly. "Man, you could have knocked me down with a straw when I saw who it was. I didn't believe it till Miss Cameron sent Mike out at the end of the first act to say you were going on in Helena's place."

"Helena!" Ginny exclaimed. "I almost forgot. Does anybody know how her father is?"

"We stopped at the hospital. They think he is going to be all right, but they won't know for sure for another 48 hours." Cappy finished his drink and rattled the ice.

There didn't seem to be anything more to say. Cappy had already talked about the play; she couldn't ask him again how he liked it. She could hardly come out with something about school. Nothing occurred to her. She had already asked about Helena. Why didn't Cappy say something? He talked so much when he was with other people!

"Want some food? There's a big mess of stuff on that table over there. Say—" Cappy's eyes were bright. "Have you met the Big Noise yet? The Broadway star?"

"I haven't even said hello to Miss Cameron herself." Ginny looked around and caught a glimpse of a sleek black dress moving into the kitchen. "I'd better—"

"Sure." Cappy was gone almost before she moved. Looking back, she saw him talking away in a little knot of people over by the window. She thought even the back of his head looked relieved. What a drag she must be!

"Ginny! My angel, my wonder child—come here!" The grip with which Ginny was becoming so familiar reached out and hauled her through the kitchen door. Ginny began to laugh. It was the same arm—Miss Cameron's arm —but this time it felt like a rescue line instead of a trap.

On the kitchen stool against the wall sat a tall, slender person. Not just a person—a famous person. There was no mistaking Miss Constance Vane! Ginny's first thought was, "She's beautiful!" and her second was, "But she's *old!*" Later, she realized she was wrong both times. Constance Vane had a sharp nose, a large and slightly crooked mouth, and a skin that needed all the powder and lipstick she put on it. And she was only in her early 40s. She wore her silver-blonde hair twisted in a huge French knot, and she held her head, on its long, slender neck, in a way that no others had so far been able to copy.

"Here's the one I especially wanted you to meet." Miss Cameron pulled Ginny forward. "Tell her what you told me."

"I shall do no such thing," the beautiful voice protested. "Do you want the child to become stuck-up?"

Miss Cameron laughed. She had put on fresh lipstick and looked quite handsome in her own way. "When you know Ginny," she told her cousin, as she piled bread and cheese on a tray and handed it to Mr. Channing through the doorway, "you will know what a joke *that* is." She took some more bottles out of the icebox and went into the living room.

In the tiny kitchen, littered with glasses and paper napkins, there was silence. "Clear off that stool and sit down," said Miss Vane at last. "Just put the glasses in the sink or some place."

Ginny lifted the glasses and had an idea. "I could just wash them up. It looks as if Miss Cameron could use a hand in here anyway." Then she went bright red. If that didn't sound for all the world as if she were telling Constance Vane she should have helped—! Bending over the sink to hide her face, she heard for the first time the warm, rich laughter that New York audiences had paid as much as ten dollars a ticket to hear.

"Quite right, my dear," Constance Vane said. "I ought to be helping. But there are things I can do and things I can't and I've made it a point all my life never to allow myself to be pushed into false positions."

Scrubbing fiercely, Ginny murmured, "I didn't mean you should—nobody would expect a famous star—"

"No, there you are wrong—Ginny, is it? I know a dozen beautiful stars who enjoy this kind of thing. When they get a chance to work around the house, they leap at it. It's not because I'm famous that I avoid it." She grinned suddenly; not a mysterious smile but a wide grin. "I just hate it. If I made my living shining shoes I would still try to pay somebody to do my house work for me. People should do what they're fit for and love to do."

Ginny set the last glass to drain and scrubbed out the sink. There were a hundred questions rushing about

her head. Did she dare ask Miss Vane any of them?

Constance Vane said, "Turn around, Ginny. Stand up. That's it—the way you stood on the stage tonight. What's the matter with your spine?"

"Nothing. I'm just so tall—"

For an answer, Miss Vane got down off the kitchen stool. Ginny stared. She was at least five-feet-ten, and she stood up straight and tall. She sat down again, smoothing the light gray dress over her long legs. "Five-two or five-ten, what matters is what you do with it on stage," Constance Vane declared. "A woman on the stage makes herself—or rather makes the character she's playing—with her own two hands, plus brains and talent.

It doesn't matter what she looks like to start with."

"Oh, I can't act!" Ginny exclaimed in horror. "I'm only a back-stage worker in the club. Tonight was an accident, my going on for Helena. I never dreamed . . ."

Miss Vane was looking at her strangely. "My cousin told me all about it. She said you were a shy sort of girl."

"Shy!" Ginny choked. "Miss Vane, I'm a *case!* Why, I couldn't think of a thing to say out in the living room with those others! I never can. I'm scared to death of people. I just can't think how I managed tonight—except I did so want the play to be a success. Miss Cameron worked so hard. I just can't understand—"

"I can." A small smile lifted Miss Vane's lips. Her blue-green eyes looked wise. "I rather think it's because you are a born actress and don't know it," she said.

Smiling, Miss Vane went on, "You were extremely good up there on stage tonight. Don't argue. You *were* Rosalind. Oh, there were rough spots. But you came through. You created Rosalind up there, and you convinced the audience they were watching her, not a girl named Ginny Harris. That's something to try and go on with, isn't it?"

Go on with? Go on where? "Do you mean—do you think I could possibly do it again?"

"If the other girl doesn't go on, you have to do it again tomorrow night anyway, don't you? No, I didn't mean that. I meant, have you ever thought about going into the theater as your work after you get out of school?"

Ginny took a deep breath. Was the woman mad? Shy people didn't decide to stand up in front of batteries of lights and expose themselves to the cruel eyes of strangers while they made fools of themselves!

Miss Vane held up a hand on which an enormous ring flashed blue-green fire. "Being shy is no handicap, Ginny. On the contrary. I could give you a list from here to London of the shy people—terribly shy—whose names are up in lights this minute! It's quite simple, really. A doctor friend of mine explains it beautifully in his new book. When you are afraid to face people, what could be better than to be able to face them not as yourself?

"On stage, you can be somebody invented by a writer. You are not even responsible. You can be free as air! You can do and say everything that's necessary. You can be strong, brave, weak, beautiful, ugly—anything, because it's not yourself you are showing. You have an excellent personality for an actress, Ginny."

She slid gracefully off the stool and put a hand on Ginny's shoulder. "Think it over. If you decide to work at it—and it will be *work*—I think you might not regret it. Well—now I've had my rest, I suppose I'd better go help in my share on the party."

As far as Ginny cared, the Drama Club party, going strong and noisy in the next room, might have moved to China. She floated on a cloud of gray silk.

"Ginny!" Miss Cameron edged into the kitchen with another batch of glasses. "Out here! You are certainly

49

not going to play Cinderella tonight!"

Ginny looked at her. "Your cousin . . ." she began.

Miss Cameron laughed. "I know. She has that effect on everybody. Move over, Ginny. You really must go back to the party. Only . . ." She paused. "Whatever Cousin Connie told you, please do listen carefully. She's absolutely sincere about the theater. And she knows what she's talking about. She thought you were great on the stage tonight. I'm sorry she won't be able to see you tomorrow night—oh, yes," she added, seeing Ginny's dismay, "you do have to go on again. Helena's staying at the hospital until they are sure her father is out of danger."

Doubt and fear rushed back over Ginny. To go on stage once and live through it was pure luck. It didn't matter what *anybody* said, she couldn't do it again.

"Oh, and another thing," Miss Cameron added, "have you ever heard of Oliver Williams? You know—the actor," Miss Cameron said.

Now Ginny remembered. Posters were up all over town telling of the new theater company, with Oliver Williams' name in large print. There had been a lot of talk about it among her sister Madeline's young friends. Brockford was right next door to Glenside, and never had there been anything like a real theater in this part of the state.

"Now, don't get excited," Miss Cameron was saying, "but Cousin Connie told me that Oliver Williams *himself* might be coming to see our play tomorrow night. And Ginny, I know he will be watching for you."

CHAPTER 5

Standing Room Only

"Me!" Ginny exclaimed. "Why would anybody come to see me?"

Miss Cameron groaned and pushed back her hair with a soapy hand. "Ginny, if only you had a drop of stage-struck blood in your veins! Don't you understand? Oliver Williams, who is even more famous than my Cousin Connie, is over in Brockford setting up what's called a permanent theater company.

"If he comes to the play, he won't be simply filling in a free evening. He will be looking us over for possible actors."

Seeing only a blank look on Ginny's face, Miss Cameron sighed. "Pay attention, and I will try to get through to you. With Cousin Connie giving you a big build-up, and with the great performance I know you are going to turn in tomorrow night, Oliver Williams might very well be interested in taking you on as an apprentice—a beginner—in his new company. How would you feel about that?"

"But what would I do?" Ginny asked.

"Act! Or rather—learn to act. Hasn't it occurred to you that you have talent?"

Ginny began to flutter. "Miss Vane did say something about my working in the theater. But she doesn't know it was just a lucky accident tonight. I could never do it again!"

"There's no use arguing with you," Miss Cameron said. "You get out there now and have some fun. We can talk about this later on."

Slowly, Ginny went back into the other room. Constance Vane was holding court on the sofa and sent Ginny a bright smile. Emmy was dancing with Cappy. Everybody, in fact, appeared to be having a whale of a time. "It's time I went home," she decided. "After all, it's been a big night. . . ."

Ginny didn't expect to close her eyes, but she slept the moment she hit the pillow. Her dreams, however, were tiring. Behind a silver-gray screen, Constance Vane sat smiling and calling, but every time Ginny tried to get through, somebody who looked like Mike Dyne and Cappy Roberts stood in front of the screen and said, "Who are you trying to kid?" Ginny was relieved to open her eyes to morning. It had been a terrible night.

In the kitchen, Mrs. Harris was just finishing breakfast. She beamed as Ginny came in. "Your father stayed as long as he could," she said, "but he had to go down and open the store. He did want to tell you how proud we were, Ginny! I had no idea you could act the way you did. You were simply marvelous. I always knew that if you got the chance . . ."

Ginny poured her juice and started a couple of eggs. Now why did her mother's praise bother her? Her mother wasn't saying anything against her. Her mother was telling her she was proud of her. It wasn't often she had reason to be.

"Now, about the summer," Mrs. Harris said happily. "The way I see it, maybe you should take some courses. In how to act, and things like that."

"Mother, for heaven's sake! This summer I'm going to get a job just the way I've planned. I have to begin earning a living!"

"People earn good money in the theater!" her mother said. "My gracious, Ginny, some make millions!"

"But one performance doesn't mean I can act!" Ginny almost wailed. She tried to gobble her eggs more quickly. What was the matter with everybody, trying to convince her she was something special? Ginny choked on her eggs. The events of the night before were coming back loud and clear. Her mother, carrying on about a stage career—that was one thing. But Miss Cameron said all

53

those nice things. The really famous, important Constance Vane took all that trouble to talk to her. And Oliver Williams might be coming to see the play tonight! Ginny jumped up.

"It's all nonsense!" she exclaimed. "Anybody who knows me knows it was just a crazy fling! I got pushed out on the stage and I went through the motions!" She stamped out before her surprised mother could reply.

Most Saturdays, Ginny worked in her father's store. But this morning, when her mother insisted she get some extra rest, she didn't argue. She lay down until the house was safely empty, then got dressed and went over to the library, telling herself, "They will find out tonight how well I can act. That is, if I get myself anywhere near the stage!"

That was the way she really felt. It was the only sensible way to feel. But she couldn't help being curious. If Oliver Williams was really so important, and if he was coming tonight to see *her*, then maybe she ought to find out more about him.

A couple of back issues of the *Brockford Signal* gave Ginny all the information she wanted. The man was a famous actor. He had an international reputation, and he was about to make Brockford a name in the world of the theater. He was going to set up a "permanent acting company." Evidently this meant that he would have a small group of actors living right there in Brockford or near it, who would work as a team—not just to put on one play, as companies did on Broadway, but to put on one play after another.

Besides these actors who would form the core of the company, Mr. Williams expected to take on a few young, unknown people and train them to act. The newspaper named some important men who had put up money for the company, and there were pictures of the large old Brockford house which had already been made over, at great expense, into a small but complete theater.

"'The whole movement of the theater today is away from Broadway,'" Mr. Williams was quoted as saying. "'It is important to bring good theater to people who have had little chance to see it. We want to build new audiences and new talent as well. Brockford offers . . .'"

Much of it Ginny did not really understand. The only stage play she had ever seen was "Peter Pan," to which she had been taken one Christmas in New York when she was too little to remember. But the stuff about "young people" and "new talent" . . . was that where Miss Cameron thought *she* might fit in? On a real stage?

She left the library with her heart going much too fast. Oliver Williams was really a big name—a top figure in the theater world. How could anyone in his right mind *imagine* that such a star would come to see a high-school play tonight, or notice Ginny Harris even if he was there!

All afternoon Ginny repeated firmly, "He won't be there!" And all afternoon she grew more frightened . . . because suppose he was? Twice she had her hand on the hall telephone, ready to call Miss Cameron and cry out that she *couldn't* go on. The first time she stopped herself by will power. The second time, just as she touched the phone, it rang. It was Emmy.

"I just got back from the ticket sale over at school. It's a mad house!" she said happily. "The whole town is over there yelling for tickets because they heard about Constance Vane being there last night and they think they may see her tonight if they get in! Some laugh. Miss Cameron told us she left town this morning. She's taking off for London tonight!"

"Thank goodness!" Ginny gasped.

"Yes, but have you heard what's even better? This guy Oliver Williams—the one who's starting that new theater over in Brockford—he's coming!"

Ginny took a deep breath. "He will never come to a high-school play. That's just silly. He's too important."

Emmy laughed. "Better tell him that. Because Miss Cameron just sent Cappy over on his little red Vespa to deliver a whole bunch of tickets to him! Our local people will really have someone to stare at tonight."

Ginny hung up with a shaking hand. It was only 5:30, but if she didn't get over to the school right this minute, something told her she would never get there at all. Maybe she could sweep or help set the stage. She could find something to do until it was time to put on Rosalind's costume. Not even Oliver Williams could bother her then. All he would see would be Rosalind!

Ginny went the long way to school, but it was still only six o'clock when she got there. The front yard was quiet, the front doors locked. When she went around to the side door, she saw that Emmy had been right. The kids at the ticket table were still being swamped by people wanting to buy tickets. As Ginny went in, Ed Wiley came out and put up a "Sold Out" sign. Underneath, it said "Standing Room Only." For a high-school play!

Coming early had been a good idea. It was hard to believe how much work was needed to make the sets fresh again after one performance! The stage crew welcomed her with glad cries, and Roz at once stuck a tube of gold paint into her hand.

"Miss Cameron said the gold on the throne didn't show up enough last night. Go do something."

The "throne" was only a strange chair that Miss Cameron had found in a junk shop for the Duke, Celia's father, to sit on in the "Duke's Court" scenes. It had looked perfectly fine last night. But nothing was going to be good enough tonight—not with the great Oliver Williams coming!

Ginny found a rag and set to work rubbing the gold cream around the chair's edges, adding a few designs of her own for good measure. When she finished, there was more gold than wood showing—surely enough even for Oliver Williams!

Capping the tube, Ginny went back to the supply room to put it away and kicked her toe against a sealed paint can that had been left in the wrong place. When she bent to shove it back she saw that it was one of the cans of liquid the crew had used on the backs of the "flats" so they wouldn't catch on fire. All the cans had been labeled to show where they were supposed to be used. Ginny frowned. This can was full, and a label was still pasted across the top: "No. 6, 7, 8 Flats." As nearly as she remembered, those were the "walls" of Rosalind's room.

"Roz!" Ginny called.

Roz hurried up. She looked at the label and swallowed. "Gosh. Are you thinking what I'm thinking? Those flats never got treated!"

Ginny was already picking a paint brush from the rack. "Don't say anything to anyone, even Miss Cameron. I will do them right now by myself," she told Roz. "Remember, when we made up the stuff, Miss Cameron said it should be used just as close to performance time as possible."

Of course she hadn't meant they should do their painting two hours before a performance! But the fire laws were extremely strict, and the Fire Department would have closed them down in a minute if they had known about the flats that were not protected.

"Ginny, you are the greatest," Roz said with feeling. She helped Ginny find flats 6, 7 and 8 where they were stored in the wings, ready to be rolled out, and left her.

It was fortunate that the stuff dried quickly. On top of

a ladder, painting away, Ginny did feel a bit like a hero. "This is what I really like," she thought. "I'm good at this, working with my hands. I will get myself through tonight somehow, and then, so help me, I will never go near a stage again. Except the back of it." But there was still tonight to get through.

CHAPTER 6

A Feeling of Loss

Tonight felt different. Both back stage and out front, as performance time came near, there was more excitement. When Emmy came back stage to help Ginny get into the purple gown, she reported that all the standing room had been sold out.

"We could play to standing room only for a week if we wanted to!" She hooked Ginny up the back.

"Everybody in Glenside likes to go some place on Saturday night," Ginny said, trying to be matter-of-fact. "It's not because this is so great."

"Well, of course not!" Emmy said. "It's all the excitement over Constance Vane last night."

Ginny stabbed herself slightly with the pin she was putting on. She would *not* think. She would *not* get sick

60

to her stomach. But what would Emmy say if she knew that the great Oliver Williams might be coming tonight to see *Ginny Harris?* Nonsense. Impossible. And it didn't matter anyway. Whoever was out there, she only had to go on and do what she had done the night before. If only —if *only* the magic would hold. Could it happen twice?

Emmy put a few more hairpins into the hair style Ginny wore for her first scenes. "I'd better go back now," she said. "You look great and I can't stand not seeing what's going on out there! I will be back to help when you change." With a quick hug, she ran out. Ginny started pacing her small room—two steps one way, two steps the other. She wasn't on in the first scene. If she went out, she would just be in the way.

Coralee put her head around the curtain. "Are you ready, too?" she asked in a weak little voice. "Should we go out, do you think? I can't just sit here."

"Come on," Ginny said. The five-minute call came as they found themselves a hidden corner, behind Mike Dyne and Phil Baynes, where they could peep out at the audience. "They're all dressed up!" Coralee whispered. "Oh, gracious—it's *worse* tonight! There are so many of them, it's like a real play. I wasn't anything like this nervous last night!"

"They're dressed up because it's Saturday," Ginny whispered back. But the huge crowd and the whole air in the hall made her as nervous as Coralee. Her stomach flipped as the orchestra started up, the lights went down, and the audience sounds began to die slowly away.

Ginny wondered if any actor, no matter how experienced he was, ever got used to the terror as the outer curtain went up and the "house tabs"—the fancy inner curtain—swept apart. Then she stopped thinking at all. The familiar lines Mike and Phil were speaking began to create the magic world of the play. They weren't even Mike and Phil any longer—they were Orlando and Adam. Ginny felt strangely calm all of a sudden, almost as though she couldn't wait to be out there.

She lost track of time. When the curtain closed upon the exit of the boys, the stage crew slid in the "Duke's Lawn," into which she and Celia would make their entrance. Ginny felt exactly as if she had been looking down on the grass from her window in the Palace and had just come down there with her Cousin Celia for their usual walk around the fountain.

The curtain opened again. Ginny waited for the clapping to die down, and started forward as she and Coralee were supposed to. Suddenly, in the opposite wing she saw Miss Cameron making fierce faces and motioning furiously, and she realized that Coralee had not come along with her. Gosh—and all of the opening words were Coralee's!

Already half way across the stage, Ginny hesitated. Then it came to her very simply. She didn't even think about it. She went all the way to the fountain, appeared to trail her hand in it, and walked slowly back toward the wing in which she could now see Coralee, her face white. Ginny smiled as though just spying her cousin, and held out her hand—and, thank heaven, somebody finally gave Coralee a little push from behind.

Moving forward, she came into audience view as she caught Ginny's hand. The first words came out—low at first but becoming more steady and clear. " 'I pray thee, Rosalind, sweet my coz, be merry'." Followed in a stage whisper by "Boy, that was close!"

It was a long, important scene. By the time Ginny left the stage, the horrible first moment was long forgotten. Miss Cameron said thankfully, "That cover job you did was worthy of a real actor!" Ginny wanted to be Rosalind and live in the "Forest of Arden" and be in love with Orlando just as long and as completely as she could.

Scene followed scene, act followed act. And then again it was time for curtain.

Ginny had a strange feeling of loss as she and Mike took their final bows. The play was over, and she didn't want it to be. In the noisy dressing room, she tried to look happy as everyone sighed with relief and exclaimed, "Am I glad that's over! Now things can get back to normal!" But for Ginny, normal wasn't good. She thought sadly that the last two days had been the best of her life.

There was no party tonight; most of those in the play had dates or were going to parties. Even Emmy had not been around when Ginny came out into the yard.

Ginny was walking along by the side of the school, avoiding the lighted front hall through which some of the audience was still coming, when somebody called her. Miss Cameron stood motioning to her from the front step.

"Come here, Ginny," she called sharply, as Ginny hesitated. There was nothing to do but go over. Mr. Channing and a few other Glenside teachers were with Miss Cameron. They all told Ginny that she had been even better than the night before.

While she was thanking them, she noticed two strangers with the group. One was a handsome older woman who was smiling at her. But it was the other who dried up Ginny's voice and made her want to run away. He was a slim man, not very tall, with a narrow, dark face, a sharp nose, and the most brilliant eyes Ginny had ever seen. Ginny's knees went weak. This had to be Oliver Williams, she knew before Miss Cameron introduced her.

All he said was, "How do you do. I thought you did a most interesting job this evening." Ginny, carried away by the sound of his British voice, almost lost the sense of the words. She finally heard Miss Cameron explain, "The poor girl's a bit nervous from the last two days. After all, she's been living the under study's dream—taking over for the star at the last minute!"

"But I wasn't a real under study," Ginny heard herself say. She wanted to bite her tongue. Now who cared about that? "I am glad to meet you, Mr. Williams," she

added. "And thank you for—for—" For what? Well, for coming. But I can't thank him for coming. He didn't come to see just me. Thank him for his compliment? But I'm not even sure what he said, and he said it too long ago, now. "Good heavens," Ginny thought in agony, feeling all eyes upon her, "what *shall* I say?"

There was no doubt about it. The magic had gone when the curtain came down. Ginny Harris was her old squeaky-voiced, shy self again!

"Miss Cameron tells me you've been thinking about the theater," Oliver Williams said. "Perhaps you would like to come along one of these days and talk to me."

Ginny found a small white business card in her hand. "Don't hurry about it," Oliver Williams said. "We will be setting things up over in Brockford for several weeks. We won't be in serious operation until the middle of August. Take your holiday or whatever you've planned this summer and think about it."

The next minute they were gone. Shaken, Ginny stood on the step until a car pulled up before her. In it were her sister Madeline and Jack, who had managed to get tickets at the last minute.

"Was that *Oliver Williams* talking to you?" Madeline demanded, moving over to make room for Ginny. "What in the world—"

"Ginny, you were great," Jack interrupted, leaning forward. "Why didn't you ever say you could act?"

"Because I can't," Ginny said weakly. "This whole

thing—honestly, it's so silly. I've never thought I could act. I couldn't possibly do anything like that."

"Oh, Ginny, for heaven's sake!" Madeline was really annoyed. "You've never given anything a thought except how to keep yourself hidden from the world. It's time you grew up! You were good tonight, and everybody we talked to said you were wonderful last night, too. And without any preparation or anything! Why shouldn't people think you may have something? Besides, we heard Miss Cameron call you over to meet Oliver Williams, and I will bet she didn't bother introducing the others."

Madeline forgot her anger. "What did he say? How did he sound? I always wondered if his voice could be as wonderful in real life as it is on TV."

"Golly, that's right!" Ginny remembered. Why, she had seen Oliver Williams on TV too. It was in a play about a year ago. How could she have forgotten that voice and personality?

"What's that?" Madeline had discovered the card in Ginny's hand. "Ginny, he didn't offer you a job!"

"Of course not!" Ginny took back the card. "He was very polite and charming and all that, and he said he had enjoyed the play."

"But didn't he say anything special—"

"Maddie, the girl's tired," Jack put in. "Give her a minute to catch her breath. You can be darn sure that Williams guy didn't fall on Ginny's neck and tell her he had been waiting for her all his life!"

"That's right, he didn't," Ginny said, giving Jack a grateful smile. If only they would all take that attitude—treat the whole thing as a nice accident that was now over and had not been all that important anyway . . . except maybe to help Ginny Harris become a little more sure of herself.

When she got up to her room, Ginny pushed the card to the very back of her desk drawer and got slowly into her nightgown. Then she took the card out and stuck it into the corner of her blotter.

"Think!" Oliver Williams had told her. If she hid the card away, it would be too easy to push the whole problem to the back of her mind and let it sink down out of sight. And she really couldn't treat it as something that didn't matter. She *did* have to think. The future was coming closer every minute. If only—if only they would let her think about it for herself!

CHAPTER 7

"I Don't Want to Try!"

The white card with Oliver Williams' name on it was there, each morning, when Ginny got up. It remained fresh and white days after "The Duke's Palace" and the "Forest of Arden" had been rolled away to be stored in Glenside High's basement. The card stayed fairly clean even through the senior dance night.

By school rule, senior dances were stag affairs, so there was no date problem. Ginny went alone, like everyone else. She was asked to dance far more than she had expected. But though her white gown was lovely, and she kept telling herself what a good time she was having, she was glad when the night was over. She was not comfortable. She never knew whether to talk or not. What did others find to say, anyway?

As she undressed that night and hung the white gown away, Oliver Williams' card caught her eye. The stage smell of paint and cold cream and dust came back to her. She remembered the sudden silence as the curtain went up—the eager way in which, from the wings, she had watched that other world come alive out on the stage.

Nothing that had ever happened to her before or since had been like that. How at home she had felt in those costumes—how sure she had been, in spite of being scared! If she called Oliver Williams . . .

Ginny came back to earth. Shoving the card into the blotter, she tied back her hair, turned out the light and went to bed. She knew what she had to do, what made sense. She had to graduate, get some kind of summer job and try to figure out the future—a practical, sensible kind of future.

Time moved faster than ever. Suddenly even graduation was over. For a few days, people who had not really been friends at school became very close as they ran around town saying good-by. Emmy went off for her last year as a camp assistant—"My last year of doing nothing," she called it. She kept trying to talk Ginny into signing up with her for business college in the fall.

There was no reason why she shouldn't. But Ginny held off. Maybe something better would occur to her during the summer. Maybe, when she finally worked up her courage and went looking for a job, she would come across something really interesting to her.

Then one night her father came home and asked her how she would like to work at Margetson's, the biggest and smartest department store in Glenside.

"I'm not just asking," he told her. "I know there's a job there if you want it. What do you think?"

Ginny knew she ought to jump at it—a job without tramping around looking for one was more than she deserved. But her very insides turned pale at the thought of selling. "I couldn't be a sales girl, Dad," she protested. "I don't think I could ever talk a total stranger into buying something . . ."

"Who said anything about selling? I happen to know there are some openings in their office." Mr. Harris shook out his newspaper and folded it with a neat crease. "You go see Mrs. Winters. They need girls to take the place of those on vacation."

As Ginny still looked in doubt, he put aside his paper. "Now look, Ginny, your mother and I are not about to push you into a job. But how is a girl going to find herself if she doesn't go out and start? There's a job there. All you have to do is to go down and ask for it!"

After all, it was not as hard as she had expected. Mrs. Winters, a thin, calm woman, nodded when she read Ginny's name on the application form. "You must be Jim Harris's daughter. I'm glad you came in to see us. Now let's see, what can you do and where can we use you?"

Ginny came away with a summer job. Nor was it all

because of her father's "connections." Mrs. Winters said she did very well on her typing test, and thought they could use her speed-writing skill as well.

Weak with success, Ginny wandered through the outer office and forgot to thank a young man who held the door for her. She wouldn't even have known he was there except that he spoke. "Get the job?"

"Yes!" Ginny said. Then she looked up. "How did you know?"

"Well, people don't come to these offices unless they are being hired—or fired. It was an easy guess." Instead of going in, he closed the door and stood in the hall looking down at her in a puzzled way. "Now don't tell me," he said. "I'm going to figure it out myself. Where did we meet?"

Ginny, who hoped she was not as red-faced as she felt, smiled up at him. She had known him at once.

He snapped his fingers. "Of course! You are the girl I almost ran over."

"And you are the bad driver," Ginny retorted. They laughed while people, hurrying past with papers and files, glanced at them curiously.

His name, he told her, was Bill Kittredge—William Turner Kittredge—and he had been going into the office because he worked here at Margetson's. He was in training, hired by Margetson's because they were interested in his possibilities as a future—"A *very* future," he said modestly—executive.

He had told Ginny all this briefly, standing in the hall outside the office. And he had added, "Tell you what— I will buy you lunch on Monday to celebrate your first day as a worker." Then he hesitated. "Unless you had other plans?"

Ginny shook her head. "How could I? I don't know another soul in this place. I'd love to."

It had been the right thing to say. That was another thing about Bill, besides his slim height and his nice voice and his warm brown eyes. You knew he was looking at you, thinking about you when he talked to you—not just a girl, but *you*. Was that what made it so easy to talk to him?

Ginny would have been much more shy on her first morning, but there were two other new girls. She didn't stand out in any way as the three were shown around and told what they were to do. Faced with so many new people, Ginny did have an attack of her old doubts. But when she did, she reminded herself that she would be with Bill for lunch.

Bill did not laugh at her fears. He took her to lunch at a little place around the corner from Margetson's, saying they could not really talk in the store lunch room. Ginny was glad, because by that time she wanted a chance to remind herself that Margetson's office wasn't the whole world. Bill watched her thoughtfully as she described her morning.

"I wouldn't worry," he said. "Anybody's nervous on his

first day. I will never forget mine. I was sure every time I passed somebody he was laughing behind my back. The fear wears off."

With Bill to help through the first strange days, Ginny grew to like working at Margetson's very much. The work was quite easy, and she did it well. The office manager, Mrs. Endel, came to depend on her much as Miss Cameron had.

And by the third week in July she had had many dates with Bill. Her first surprise at how comfortable she was with him had worn off, and she now expected to have a good time when they went out together. In fact, her whole life was taking a nice, comfortable shape, with nothing new or challenging to disturb her.

One evening, just before closing time, Mrs. Endel asked Ginny to leave some bills with the jewelry-department office on her way out. Bill was picking her up for dinner and an early movie, so she decided, to save time, to leave from the front entrance, rather than the employee's door at the back. As she joined the customers leaving the store in answer to the closing bell, somebody exclaimed, "Ginny Harris! I was just thinking about you!"

It was Miss Cameron. She slipped her arm through Ginny's and fairly pulled her along, talking so fast Ginny didn't have to say anything. In the ten yards before they reached the door, Ginny learned that Miss Cameron had just come back from Mexico and that she was going up to Cape Cod to spend the rest of the summer working as the director of a small summer-theater group.

They were outside now, and Miss Cameron stopped to give Ginny a questioning look. "Which reminds me, I thought I'd be hearing from you about the Brockford Playhouse, Ginny. How did you make out there?"

Ginny swallowed. "Well, I—I haven't done anything about it, Miss Cameron. I'm working here, for the time being." She saw Bill pulling up to the curb. "Please come and meet a friend of mine," she said, hoping to change the subject.

Miss Cameron greeted Bill, but went on at once, "What happened, Ginny? Oliver Williams was really interested. I can't believe you'd rather work here at Margetson's than have a chance at a real career!"

Ginny looked down at her shoes. "I'm not selling. I'm in the office. I—I think I like it here."

There was a pause. Then Miss Cameron took Ginny's hand. "I don't know why I thought those two days on the stage would change your whole personality. But Ginny dear, honestly—you can't *still* be so scared of everything— especially not of the theater! Not after the job you did! You must give yourself a chance! Oh, dear—" She glanced at her watch. "I'm keeping the two of you, and I have to be off myself. Ginny, give me a ring and we will talk about this." She said a polite good-by to Bill Kittredge and hurried off.

There was nothing for Ginny to do but tell Bill the whole story about the play—which meant telling him the

story of her life, more or less. He kept saying, "But Ginny
—*any* girl would have been surprised, being pushed on
to the stage like that!" The more she tried to explain to
him what a double shock it had been to a girl as shy as
she was, the more he shook his head.

"I hear you, but I don't believe you," he said. "Of
course I know you are not the most forward girl in the
world, but I've never noticed you had any trouble being
with people."

"I never do, with you." Ginny sighed. "But believe
me, Bill, there have been times when I simply couldn't
get a word out in the most ordinary situations. In class,

even. Or with people I'd known for years and years."

"But what about dates?" Bill asked. "Surely if a boy invited you to go out you knew he wanted to be with you —so how could you be shy of him?"

Ginny blushed. As close as she was beginning to feel to Bill, as friendly and as comfortable, she still knew it wasn't exactly necessary to burst out that before he came into her life there had hardly been any dates. "I think Margetson's has helped a lot," she said. "I still get butterflies if Mrs. Endel sends me out to another office. But when it's just between me and my typewriter, I really feel as if I can do a good job."

"I should hope so, because I know you are doing one," Bill said. "But why should you give Margetson's a thought when you have this other possibility? You must have been pretty special out on that stage, Ginny, from the way that Cameron woman talked. Gosh, you must know it yourself! You don't think a guy like Oliver Williams goes around inviting every high-school senior he meets to come and try out!"

Ginny was annoyed to find her voice shaking. "That's just the point—he hardly even met me! How was he to know that the whole thing was simply an accident that could never happen again?"

"How do you know what he saw up there?" Bill answered, motioning the waiter to bring the check. "Who are you to say it was just an accident?"

"Because I know Ginny Harris!" Ginny shot back in

77

a voice that made heads turn as they left the restaurant. In a lower tone she added, "Why should I try for something I know I'm not good enough to get, Bill? Why should I blow myself up with a lot of crazy hopes and then come down to earth? I'd rather stay down and not get my heart broken."

Bill took her hand. "All right. I won't nag you about it, Ginny. If you honestly don't want to try—well, that's it. Just promise me you'll think about it once more, just to be sure that you aren't too scared to give it a try."

Ginny was quiet in the car. Had she hoped for more understanding from Bill? Had she wanted him to say, "Now, now, of course you don't have to stick your neck out if you don't want to. Of course it's all right for you to settle down in a nice quiet job."?

She must have wanted something other than the argument he had given her, because she was more upset than she had been since the night Oliver Williams had given her his card. That card! She knew darn well that it was still there, though now she never let herself think about it.

Feeling her mood, Bill didn't talk much, either. But when they turned into Main Street, he laughed. "Isn't this *our* corner?" he asked. "The spot where I almost broke your leg?"

Ginny looked out. "Yes, right here." She smiled, too, and the ice was broken. "Don't you remember how I ran away from you that time? That's what I was trying to explain about myself—how frightened I've always been of any contact with people, especially a new person. Didn't you think I was some kind of a nut?"

"Not really. I thought you were—well, rather young, and I thought you put me down as being out for a pick-up. No, I didn't think you were a nut at all." He nodded toward the Y as they passed it. "I often wondered—were you coming from that dance they had here? In something called The Pumpkin Room? I heard the music when I went by."

Ginny explained about The Pumpkin Room, including the fact that it was called The Pumpkin Room because it closed at twelve sharp—the hour at which Cinderella's coach changed back into a pumpkin. "It has strict rules," she explained, "because it's for young people."

Bill grinned. "We are still young. Why don't we go some time?"

"It's not open during the summer," Ginny said. "And besides . . ." She paused. Why—she couldn't go! All during high school she had thought about going, and planned that one day she would get up the courage to go, and now . . . "Now I can't go," she said, in wonder. "Once you've graduated from high school it's not open to you any more! Oh, Bill—I never went, not once, and now I can't go even if I want to!"

It was hardly the end of the world. Ginny didn't mean to sound as though it were. But all at once it seemed like a great loss—something important she had missed and now would never have a chance at again. Bill took one hand from the wheel and put it over hers for a minute. "Never mind. We will show them. We can go to the Brock House Roof and dance to real music. But listen, Ginny, you just said something very important. Things don't wait around for you. Sometimes you can get a chance to do something, but if you don't take it when it's there—well, maybe when you decide you do want it, it won't be around any more."

He patted her hand and put his own back on the wheel. Bill's words stayed clear and sharp in Ginny's ears. She knew exactly what he meant. She had a chance with Oliver Williams to learn to act. How did she know that, two years from now, she wouldn't be kicking herself for not having taken advantage of it?

That night, when she got home, she sat right down and wrote a note to Oliver Williams, reminding him who she was and asking for an appointment.

CHAPTER 8

Fireworks

On Saturday morning, exactly a week later, Ginny stood before a white-painted building that looked like an old Southern home. She wished with all her heart that she were anywhere else.

"I should have asked Bill to come with me," she thought for the tenth time since the Brockford bus had put her down on the corner. "At least he would have made sure I got myself through that door."

It was a big double door, with a glass front. Through it, Ginny could see that the original entrance hall had been made larger so that there was no mistaking what it was—the entrance of a theater. In fact, there was no mistaking it anyway. At either side of the glass doors, posters announced "Brockford Community Playhouse—Director, Oliver Williams," together with a list of the plays that would be presented during the months to come. There was also a list of players.

Ginny felt hot and cold and weak at the knees. Who was she to imagine that her name could ever possibly be included there?

She was half turned, ready to head back to the bus stop, when a girl carrying two pails and a brush with a long handle came through and motioned with her head for Ginny to open the door.

"Thanks a lot," the girl said, setting down the pails with relief. "I don't know why they have to send a girl to do a man's work." She looked at Ginny curiously. "Can I help you?"

"Mr.—Mr. Williams," Ginny said. "I have an appointment." Now she would have to go through with it!

The girl grinned. She had bright blue eyes and red-brown hair that shone in the sun like polished pennies. "You are an actress," she said, holding out her hand. "Welcome to the group. I'm Toni Foster. And listen— what are you nervous about? At least you have an appointment. I had one, too, when I came to try out—but you ought to see the kids that come around just hoping he will hear them read!"

Ginny's sinking feeling grew stronger. "Are there lots of girls who want to get in?"

"Are you kidding? To make a start in a brand-new company with Oliver's reputation behind it?" Toni Foster rolled her eyes. "Of course, I sometimes wonder what I'm getting a start in." She nodded toward the pails. "With dancing lessons and speech lessons and helping out with the clean-up work in my odd moments—if any—I don't know that you can call what we do around here being actors."

She grinned. "But I'd scrub floors, and I guess you would too, for the chance. Look—just go round the side here . . ."

Ginny followed directions around to the side of the building and found her way through what was evidently the stage door. It led through a bare passage lined with small lockers. At the end of it were a number of doors. Toni had told her to knock on the one marked *Office*. Ginny tapped softly, hoping she would not be heard. But the door swung open. Inside, large as life, Oliver Williams leaned against a desk and looked at her with a frown.

There seemed to be a crowd with him, but when Ginny calmed down a bit she saw that it was only two men, one of whom had opened the door and now stood with his foot against it. The other was folding up large pieces of material and pushing them into a big brown envelope. To Ginny's eyes, they both looked exactly like Oliver Williams. Was he three people?

"Oh, of course—it's you. Come in." Oliver Williams looked at the men in the room with him. "Get the estimates on those curtains and we will go on from there." He nodded, and the men went out. Ginny was alone with

him, wishing harder than ever that she had never come, never written the letter, never heard of the Drama Club at Glenside High.

But in the end, like so many things she had spent time dreading, the actual interview turned out to be almost easy. Oliver Williams was interested in only one thing: his theater. Did Ginny belong with it, or didn't she— that was all he cared to find out about her. As he asked questions, his dark eyes seemed to be looking into her brain for more information than he could find.

Was he really listening to her at all? He asked, "Now, apart from the Shakespeare effort in which I saw you, what other work have you done?"

Ginny licked her dry lips. "That—that was the first time I was ever on a s-stage in my whole life," she said.

Mr. Williams folded his arms and looked at her. "But you can act," he commented. "What's wrong with you?" He looked really interested now.

Ginny took a breath. "I'm scared," she heard herself say. Well—that's done it, she thought. Might as well let him have the whole thing, now. "I'm scared to death. Of everything. I never thought I'd live through that performance you saw. I'm scared all the time of what people are thinking about me."

"Who isn't?" Oliver Williams asked coolly. Ginny's mouth opened. He nodded. "I mean it, Ginny. Everyone suffers doubts—don't you think otherwise. It's a difference of degree, that's all. Generally one can learn to control it and gather confidence and grow out of it, after a time." He smiled his sudden, bright smile, "But you weren't scared when you were Rosalind, were you?"

Ginny said slowly, "No, I wasn't. Rosalind was—another person. Even if she was supposed to be silly or clumsy or whatever, it wasn't *me*."

Oliver Williams reached up and ran his hand over a shelf of books on the wall behind his desk. Pulling one down, he found the place he wanted and marked it with a strip of paper. "Come on," he said. "Talk will get us nowhere. Let's get along and see what you can do with Ibsen."

Ginny found herself carried along in his wake past the dressing-room doors, around corners—and then she suddenly realized she was out on a stage. *The* stage. It was plain and bare, except for a few folding chairs at one end, but the part where the audience would sit seemed to be well decorated, all blues and golds.

She had no time to examine it. Oliver Williams thrust the book into her hand.

"Now," he said rapidly, "your name is Nora. You are married to a stuffy business man who isn't as important as he thinks he is. He believes all women should be treated like children, or like possessions. He is prepared to provide his wife with a good home, nice clothes, and a treat now and then, but he simply does not understand that she has any right to a life of her own. Nora wants terribly to express some of her thoughts and ideas, but at this time—this is the nineteenth century—most people think as her husband does. Women are not supposed to have any brains."

Ginny heard him in wonder. "So," he finished, "that's who you are. Now read me this speech, please." He ran lightly down the steps to a seat in the middle of the theater and called, "Any time you are ready."

Ginny stood exposed and helpless under a bright ceiling light. Toni Foster came and perched on the arm of a seat, and several other dim figures were spotted around, watching her. Her knees were trembling and she felt sick to her stomach. Almost without knowing it, she began to read.

"Start over, please," came Oliver Williams' voice. "I can't hear you."

Ginny's throat hurt. She knew she had been forcing her voice, which was all wrong. This time, lost in Nora's words, she read to the end.

When she finished, there was a murmur from the others. "Not at all bad," she heard Oliver Williams say, and somebody else said, "How old is she—seventeen or so? Very nice for a start, I'd say."

Ginny stood there until Toni Foster came over to the

stage and helped her down. Leading her to where Oliver Williams sat, Toni gave Ginny's hand a squeeze and disappeared. Ginny stood silently until Oliver Williams told her to sit down.

"If you want to work in the theater, I think you can start with us," he said. She couldn't believe she was hearing straight. "Money and arrangements and all that—I will turn you over to John Pauling in a minute. He's our business end."

He smiled. "If you were the ordinary stage type, I'd have to give you my little stock speech to warn you that your name will not be in lights in three weeks. But you have never thought about your name in lights, so you save me all that bother. Good luck, Ginny. Glad to have you with us."

Going home on the bus, Ginny sat filled with excitement and confusion. It almost couldn't have happened. Could any girl be this lucky—without even trying?

Somehow, her parents weren't the ones she wanted to tell first. Her sister Madeline? Heaven forbid—she'd be planning a big party in a minute, to announce her sister's "career." Miss Cameron . . . if only she were here! Bill? That was the one. He worked half a day on Saturday— that was one of his extra privileges, he always said, as a "training executive."

Ginny ran into the house, threw down her purse and called Margetson's number without stopping for breath. She got Bill at the moment he was leaving. "I did it!" She began. "And what do you think happened?"

"Don't tell me," Bill said. "You walked into Oliver Williams' office and you started to shake so hard you shook your bones out of place and he had to send you home in an ambulance."

"Listen! He took me on! Oh—Bill, can you meet me right away so I can tell you all about it?"

Bill's voice sounded funny. "Gosh, Ginny, I'm sorry. I can't right now. I'm supposed to meet someone in ten minutes—let me call you later."

Ginny felt exactly as if he had emptied a pail of cold water over her head. She said stiffly, "Of course," and hung up. "It doesn't matter," she told herself. "It's not important. Why shouldn't Bill have a date with some other girl? I don't own him. We are friends. Other girls have lots of friends. It's not Bill's fault if I only have him."

But it *was* important. Creeping up to her room, Ginny realized how much she had begun to take Bill for granted. She—who had never had a boy friend before! Just because he was nice, and friendly, and liked people . . . just because he was the only boy she had ever been able to be at ease with!

Bill did call at 5:30. Without thinking, Ginny checked the hall clock when she heard his voice. He hadn't been in much of a hurry! "Ginny! I thought I'd never get away. This lunch lasted forever, and then I had to drive someone to the station, and everything took hours and hours—but never mind all that. What happened?"

"Well, I told you," Ginny said. "Mr. Williams took me on as a beginner." It sounded awfully flat, but that was how she felt, by now. "It hardly pays anything at all, but I will be learning."

"Oh, I've known kids in summer stock companies who paid for the chance to learn," Bill said. "And they weren't working with people as important as Oliver Williams! Were you scared? Did you have to read for him? How did you come through?"

Ginny bit her lip. If only she had been able to tell him when it had happened! Of course, he was still a friend— one shared one's joy with friends. But when she had called him earlier she had wanted to share it with him in a special way, because she had been stupid enough to think he was a very special friend. So much for that!

She took a deep breath. "He's terribly handsome," she said. "I think it's a waste that he should be planning to direct and produce from now on instead of being in plays himself."

Bill made a sound like a groan. "Ginny Harris, I don't want to hear about Oliver Williams—I want to hear about *you!* He's already got all the press agents he needs! Will you please—"

"Ginny, ask Bill over for dinner!" came Mrs. Harris's voice from the kitchen.

"I heard that, and I will be there," Bill said. "What time?" When Ginny hesitated, he added in a different tone, "Or doesn't the invitation come from both of you?"

"I am being a pill!" Ginny thought. "Of course it does! from both of us, Bill! Can you be here at 6:30?"

He was there five minutes early, with a great bouquet of red roses. Ginny hurried off into the kitchen to arrange them in a bowl for the table.

"He doesn't owe me a thing," she scolded herself. "From now on, I'm going to stop feeling as though he's anything special in my life!"

During dinner, she let the others do the celebrating. Her father kept repeating, "You see, Ginny, I've always said you could do anything you wanted to!" Her mother heaped food on Bill's plate as if he were her favorite son. Or son-to-be. Why, they both treated Bill as if he were a member of the family!

Ginny could hardly wait for coffee and the end of the meal. Bill suggested a drive afterward.

He headed the car toward Brockford. "I want to see this magic place," he said. "I want to be able to imagine your slaving away in it. Washing windows." She had told about meeting Toni Foster at one of the "odd jobs" that she too would probably have to do.

Ginny smiled stiffly. She almost said, "I hope I'm not taking you away from something you'd rather be doing." Not saying that, she couldn't seem to think of anything else. This was terrible. It had finally happened. It was just as hard now to talk to Bill as it had been with all the other boys. What was wrong with her, anyway?

The Playhouse was empty, of course, when they got there, but Bill pulled into a parking space behind it and they sat looking at it in silence. "It's a wonderful location," he said finally. "It ought to be a great success."

"Yes," Ginny said.

Bill looked down at her. "What's the matter, Ginny? Don't you really want to do it, is that it?"

"Oh—no, it's not the theater. I mean, of course I want to. It's just—it's all so crazy. I can't believe I actually stood up there and read for a famous actor and he said I was good enough to work with his group."

Remembering the bare, scratched stage and the eyes out there watching her, she sat up straight. "It was funny," she said slowly. "Just like the other time. I was scared out of my wits, then I saw I was supposed to be somebody named Nora and—well, I started reading, and I *was*. I'm honestly beginning to think that when I get out on a stage something happens. I—" She sat back. "But you don't really want to hear about all this, all over again."

"Why not?" Bill asked.

"Well, because . . ." Ginny trailed off into miserable silence. "It's all about me," she added after a time. "You've got plenty of other things on your mind."

Bill looked confused. "How did you know? As a matter of fact—I had a bit of good news today, too. I had a late lunch with Mrs. Winters and Mr. Warner—you know, the general manager. Starting next month, I'm going to be Mrs. Winters' official assistant. How about that?"

Ginny stared at him, her eyes shining. "You had lunch with Mrs. Winters? Why didn't you tell me who it was? Oh, Bill, it's marvelous about the job, but why didn't you just say—"

Bill had both her hands in his, and he was laughing. "Ginny! Is that what's been bothering you all night?"

Unable to speak, Ginny nodded. She felt like a fool. Bill said quietly, "I haven't dated any other girl since I met you, Ginny. If I do ever want to, I will tell you. But in the meantime—" He took her hands again. "In the meantime, here we are. If it's all right with you."

"That must mean we are going steady," Ginny thought. She felt as though the sky beyond Bill's shoulder were lit up with fireworks. What a day! Why—if Bill really did like her that much, then anything could happen! She really could go into the Brockford Playhouse and try to become an actress! It could really happen!

CHAPTER 9

A New Kind of School

"I'm going steady!" Ginny said softly to her mirror when she got upstairs that night. It didn't sound real, that way. She said it a few more times and then changed it around. She went to sleep telling herself, "Bill doesn't want to date anybody but me!" That sounded right. That made it something between herself and Bill.

Ginny needed the feeling that she wasn't alone. She needed Bill's strength and confidence to draw on during the next few weeks. There were times when, without that, she might have gone running back to her typewriter at the store.

Learning to act was *work*. And not always pleasant work. Ginny was shaken to her shoes the first time Oliver Williams was really sharp with her in a speech class.

"I expect to be told when I'm wrong," she said to Bill afterward. "I'm there to learn. But does he have to be so mean about it?" She didn't tell Bill that she had actually burst into tears.

"Just remember you are there to learn, and forget the rest," Bill advised. "He's not being mean on purpose. If he doesn't catch you up on what's wrong, how will you learn to be better?"

Next to Bill, Toni Foster was the greatest help to Ginny. Though she was only three years older, she was years ahead in experience of all kinds. She had grown up in New York City and had been interested in the stage all her life.

"This is my make-or-break time," she told Ginny one morning between lessons, as they sipped lemonade out on the back steps of the Playhouse. "I can't go on hoping too much longer—I'm not the type. If we are successful here, and if I'm good enough to be kept on, fine. But if not, I'm through, period."

Without Toni as a guide, it would have been weeks before Ginny could have figured out how the Playhouse was set up. Each day, new people appeared, going in and out of Oliver's office, taking him out to lunch in small, noisy, foreign cars with New York or California license plates.

After a while, Ginny knew who really belonged. Clay Ford and Gary Barnaby were juniors, several steps above new students like herself and Toni. They had had real experience in the theater. When they went into production on a real play, Clay would probably get a chance to design the set.

"He's never done it before for money," Toni explained, "but he's loaded with talent. Good thing, too. He and Gary are too much the same type for Oliver to need them both as actors."

Amanda Massey, who did not arrive to stay in Brockford until a week after Ginny was taken on, turned out to be the handsome older woman who had been with Oliver that night at the high school. She would play older-woman parts.

Ginny discovered that it was only her somewhat lined face and her curly gray hair that gave away Amanda's age. She had started her career dancing, and her body was as slim and firm as a girl's.

It was Amanda who taught the modern-dance exercise group which Oliver insisted everyone join. He claimed that dancing was the best way for the older ones to stay in shape, and for the young ones, like Ginny, to learn how to move around on stage.

Selena Bryce was the only one of her fellow workers whose name Ginny recognized. She was a beautiful brunette, in her 40s according to Toni, but to Ginny's eyes looking closer to 30. She had made some reputation on Broadway before going to Hollywood.

It was from her movies, of course, that Ginny knew her name. All during August, Selena flew in for two days each week. Each time, she swept Toni and Ginny into one of the dressing rooms and gave them lessons in how to make up for the stage. Toni already knew a good deal about this art, but to Ginny it was surprising that she could make herself look like a little girl or, by putting lines and shadows in certain places, could add 20 years to her age.

"This is just the beginning," Selena promised. "Later on, I will show you how to make yourselves up to help you really create the person you are playing. Out of these jars and tubes and brushes will come a thousand faces— healthy, sick, wicked, kind, hopeful—whatever you need to be. After that, of course, it's up to you to go on and *be* it."

The other big name, of whom Ginny had not heard, because he had never made a movie, was an actor named David Wainsford. To Bill, Ginny described him as "quite old," but around the Playhouse she never dared to think of him that way because it was plain that he considered himself quite young.

These were the backbone of the Brockford Playhouse. Special people—actors, orchestra men, people to design costumes—would be hired as they were needed.

"That's until we really get established," Toni explained. "Oliver has big ideas for this thing, you know. If we make money at all this year, he's going to build up a big permanent company, and even start a real drama school—not just for us, but for other kids who are serious about learning to act and going on the stage."

Ginny was paid a tiny salary, less than half of what she had earned at Margetson's. This would go on until she could draw "practice pay"—when and if she was cast in a play. That wasn't much either, according to Toni. She herself lived as cheaply as possible at a Y.W.C.A.

"When our first production is a smash, you and I will take a tiny apartment together," she told Ginny, as if it were all decided. Then, in her usual Toni manner, grinned. "Or else you'll have to borrow from your family to get me back to New York."

Besides the speech and movement classes, Ginny, Toni and Clay and Gary had classes to learn how to act. Oliver would assign them plays to study and talk about, scenes to act out. Sometimes, he would just toss out short descriptions—"You are a scared young bride meeting her husband's family" or "You are a boy who has found out that his father is a crook."

Just like that, with a wave of his hand, he would get one of them up before the others to build a whole scene out of his words. Ginny was impressed by the way the others managed, so much that when Oliver called for criticism she had nothing to say. Gradually, she did begin to see ways in which Clay or Gary could have improved a performance, but when Oliver asked for comments . . . well, it was Glenside High all over again.

Several times, when Oliver said, "Ginny, what do you think?" she bit her lips and said, "I—I thought it was fine." Her heart would stop pounding only when Oliver's eyes went on to one of the others. One day, when Gary and Toni did a little scene together, Ginny saw very clearly that Gary was not being the character he was supposed to be. But when Oliver called on her, she flushed and murmured, "I thought Toni was just right." There was a pause. Oliver's eyebrows went up. "Yes?" he said, waiting.

Ginny shook her head. Suddenly, Oliver's face went dark with anger. "Now look here," he said in a cold rage. "We aren't an audience at a free show. We are supposed to be here helping one another. If you have nothing more to offer than a nod of your head, I don't think you are in the right place! You must see *something* that needs improvement!"

Ginny gasped. A voice came out and it was every bit as furious as Oliver's. Could it be her voice? "I don't see why I have to hurt people's feelings!" she shouted. "If yours had ever been hurt you'd know how it feels!" She was shaking with anger.

"Well, that's more like it," Oliver said in his normal, smooth tones. "I rather thought we could get you to speak up sooner or later. Now listen. We haven't time for that nonsense. It's our business to learn how to do our very best work. If you have something to say that will help Gary do a better job, say it! If we don't agree, we will argue about it. That's the way we all learn."

"Well then," Ginny began, "Gary is supposed to be a rough sort of man. When he loses his temper, he should

do more than just yell at Toni. I mean a person like that wouldn't just use words." Ginny frowned. "He would hit something or throw something."

Oliver looked pleased. "You mean you feel violence in the character that ought to come out somehow in what he does."

"Yes, that's just it!" Ginny flushed with pleasure. They played the scene with Gary smashing his fist at one point on the table in front of Toni, and everybody agreed it was much better. Ginny was happy at having made a useful criticism. But she still thought, "I will never live through it when they tell me what I'm doing wrong."

Yet she was learning more than she realized, for when

Oliver did begin to make her perform, it was like being on the stage. When the others offered their comments, she had no feeling that they were finding fault with her —only with the person she was supposed to be.

As September came closer, Ginny found herself most at home in these classes. She still felt somewhat out of place with the other people, except for Toni. But when she was actually working, she was so wrapped up in what she was doing that nothing bothered her.

On her dates with Bill, she talked about nothing but the Playhouse, stopping every few minutes to let him comment and then thinking of something else she simply had to tell him. She didn't appreciate until afterward how patient he was. He seemed to find the Playhouse as thrilling as she did.

"You are certainly in the right place, Ginny," he told her. "Do you know that lately you've been all lit up like a Christmas tree? You are a different girl—not that I don't like this one even better than the other one," he added hastily.

Then, as Ginny was settling into a kind of pattern, with classes and practice performances, everything turned upside down. There was a big meeting one afternoon in Oliver's office, jammed with worried-looking men who had never been around before. Long-distance phone calls were going in and out. "Money trouble," Toni said wisely. "You wait and see."

Sure enough, when the worried men had gone, Oliver

called everyone into his office and made an announcement. Most of the money to support the Playhouse was coming from a wealthy group that supported many kinds of projects. But some of it was coming from private people, and they had suddenly decided that the Playhouse must prove itself.

"So instead of a careful, sound preparation, with plenty of time for training in working as a group, we are going to have to take a running jump," Oliver said.

"Let's make it the best job we can do, even if we aren't being given a proper chance to do it!"

Only slowly did it dawn on Ginny that he was talking about a play—not weeks away, or months away, but in as short a time as they could get one ready for production. The play had already been chosen, the wheels were already turning. The writer was to come in on Saturday.

Ginny's confusion grew. Here was the nice little world in which she was only beginning to feel happy and safe —all whirling around like laundry in a washing machine. And then Oliver threw his real bomb shell.

"I want Amanda and David back here tonight," he said. "Oh—you too, Ginny. There's a part for you."

CHAPTER 10

"I Can't Go On"

The play was called *Top of the Hill*. There was a hill in it, all right—in fact there was only one other place in it, the shabby kitchen of a small house.

"Where is the house supposed to be?" Ginny asked shyly, after she and the others had read the play that night in Oliver's office.

"Anywhere," Oliver said, as if that explained it. Ginny sat back, afraid to say more. David Wainsford put his long, thin hand to his forehead.

"Oh, *no*," he moaned. "It's one of those modern things. Oliver, we can't." He tossed his copy of the play on Oliver's desk. "It's so modern it doesn't even have conversation! I tell you, Oliver, if we do this thing, the Playhouse will be through before it starts."

"It's got plenty of conversation," Amanda Massey objected. "Look, pages and pages of talk—and some lovely juicy bits for you, David dear."

Ginny looked through her copy again. There certainly were lines and lines of talk—less for her, to be sure, than for the others, but plenty. Only, as far as she could see, it was talk that went round in circles and said nothing.

In the play, she would be a young girl named Bonnie, who lived with her widowed mother in this kitchen. Sometimes she went off to the top of a hill near the house to be alone. She was lonely and sad, but the play did not seem to say why. After a while, David appeared, a man with whom her mother had once been in love. As nearly as Ginny could see, the idea that her mother had ever been in love so shocked Bonnie that one day she walked up her hill, down the other side, out of sight, and disappeared from the stage. This was the end of the play.

Ginny did not know for sure what David meant by calling it "modern," but she agreed with his feeling against it. Amanda, however, sided with Oliver. She found it interesting and different. "And also," she added with a smile at Oliver, "cheap to put on."

Oliver brushed back his hair with a gesture Ginny was coming to know. "Thank heaven, one of you has a business head," he said. "Of *course* that's important. This thing has two sets, which will cost very little to build. Bonnie wears one dress throughout the thing—or one pair of slacks—we can figure that out. The mother has practically no costume changes. David's wardrobe will be about the most expensive item—and I think he's probably got most of it in his closet this minute.

"Further," Oliver went on, "Gordon Tyler, who wrote it, had a smash in New York last season. His name is known. And it happens that he is a relative of one of the richest men who is supporting the Playhouse.

"So now you see that I haven't chosen *Top of the Hill* because I've lost my mind. I may lose it before this is over, but for right now you must all help me not to. Shall we get on?"

They "got on." Working on a real play was not at all like working in the happy confusion of a Glenside High production. It was more like taking part in a battle plan. Oliver did not work in confusion; he worked in a steady way that seemed to drive straight for a goal. Even when, during a practice, he called out sharply, "Not that way, Ginny, you are *sad*—not sleep-walking," his words did not frighten her.

In Ginny's scenes with Amanda, Amanda always seemed to be helping her, making her sound better. But David had a way of getting between her and the front of the stage, or of moving while she was speaking, which made her nervous.

There was one very important speech of hers, during which he leaned against the kitchen table and lit a cigarette. Ginny could always see this out of the corner of her eye and it took her mind off what she was saying.

One day it bothered her so much that she got lost in the middle of a sentence. Ginny was proud of having learned her part quickly and well. Now the match flame and the movement of David's hand over in the corner suddenly dried up her words. Without thinking, she walked over, took the cigarette out of David's hand, and squashed it flat in the ash tray. When she realized what she had done she couldn't believe it.

"I'm—I'm sorry!" she gasped. Turning to Oliver, out in the theater, she repeated, "I'm sorry, Oliver. But it bothers me so! Of course I have no right to—"

Oliver had left his seat and was looking up at them from the foot of the stage. "You have every right, and don't spoil it by saying anything else," he snapped. "Your feelings are perfect. You are too young and green to know it, but our friend here was playing a very old trick on you. He has been up-staging you for days."

Ginny looked blank. David, who had first gone white with anger, now looked very much ashamed of himself. "I'm afraid it's true," he said. "I ought to deny it, but I'm too ashamed. You see, Ginny—" he turned his charming smile on her—"when an actor wants to take the attention of the audience away from the other actors, all he has to do is make some movement to catch their eye."

David took Ginny's hand. "I have a mean, nasty nature, love, but really I promise—I will never do this to you again."

Ginny would have believed anything he said, with all

that charm turned on. As they went back to their places, Amanda added, "I hope that doesn't mean you are thinking up something else to do, David dear, because mother is watching!"

Telling Toni about it afterward, during a coffee break, Ginny wondered how she had ever had the nerve. It seemed to have happened because David was interfering with the movement of the play, and that gave her the courage to be angry.

The two girls had made their instant coffee on an electric plate Amanda kept out at the stage-door desk, and Oliver happened to come by as Ginny was trying to explain. He stopped, which made her go silent and shy. Oliver still scared her a little.

"I said your feeling was good," he nodded. "It's the play that matters, Ginny. Toni, pay attention. This is a lesson. No true actor is up on the stage to show himself off. He's there to work as part of a team—to work with the other actors to make something which none of them can do alone. Real acting means team work—playing to each other. David knows that perfectly well."

Oliver grinned. "It's just that he really does have a nasty nature and sometimes it gets out of hand." He buttoned his well-cut jacket and went on out.

"Will I ever understand theater people?" Ginny wondered out loud. Toni laughed.

"You *are* one, Ginny." Her face clouded. "More of one than I am, anyway—right now."

Ginny felt ill at ease. Ever since Oliver had cast Ginny in *Top of the Hill*, Toni had changed. She was just as friendly, but not as cheerful. And she no longer seemed to feel that Oliver could do no wrong.

Ginny wondered if Toni had wanted her part as Bonnie. It wasn't her type. Toni was flashing, bright, not at all like the quiet, rather dim Bonnie. But that was all a challenge to an actress, Ginny now knew—to be able to play a character completely unlike herself. Toni never said anything, so Ginny never brought it up.

Still, there was no time for worrying about Toni. There was no time for anything but work. Three weeks was all they had before opening night! Already Ginny's mother had cut out notices in the local newspapers, the ones in which Ginny's name was mentioned. More new people appeared around the Playhouse. An older woman, Ellen Harper, acted as Oliver's secretary and assistant. Gordon Tyler, the writer, was a big young man who needed a haircut and kept chewing the stem of a pipe which never seemed to be lighted. A stage crew began its job of working with the sets and lighting.

The dressing rooms were furnished now. Ginny was given one for the run of the play—it had a mirror framed all around in lights, like the ones she had seen in the movies!

There was one horrible day when Ginny came through the stage door and was met by a young man with red hair and glasses and a camera around his neck.

"There you are!" he exclaimed, "I'm from the paper in—"

Ginny pulled away without actually hearing where he was from. That moment, Oliver had come by and the young man was drawn along the passage and turned over to Miss Harper. Ginny had to sit at her dressing table to get over the fright. A newspaper man! Golly, would she have to talk to *newspaper men*? Why, she would never be able to handle that! What did you say or do? Anyway, why would they want *her*?

The next day she found out. Madeline drove over in

great excitement with three copies of the *Brockford Signal* under her arm, and showed the Harrises a story called, "Local Girl in Williams' Play."

Miss Harper had managed to make the story mostly about the play itself, though there was still mention of "talented Ginette Harris, one of the lights of Glenside's Drama Club before her graduation in June." Somewhat wiser now in the ways of the theater, Ginny knew that without this kind of newspaper story, you didn't sell as many tickets. Stories were to let people know, and to make them want to come and see. All Ginny hoped was that men from the newspapers would leave her alone.

Yet, secretly, Ginny knew that if she had to, she could get through even a newspaper interview now without being too scared. She really was changing. It must be confidence in herself, she decided.

A certain amount of confidence even stayed with her now when she was off the stage. She was able to sit around and drink coffee with the others. She didn't feel, as she used to back in school, that people around her were talking a language she would never understand.

"If it weren't for that opening night coming so close, I'd be happy," Ginny told Bill. "But how can you forget a thing like that hanging over you? David is forever complaining that the show is bound to fall on its face, but the others tell me he's always an old lady about openings.

"I try not to listen. Amanda has no nerves, but she says that's bad. And that's why, *she* says, she will always be just a half-good actress, never the very best.

"It's Oliver who is really a wreck. He's lost all his tan and he sort of seems smaller, all pinched in with worry. Also, he won't let the others see a run-through of the play. Toni says that's a bad sign. Selena Bryce is having fits about it, but Toni and I heard Oliver tell her the other night that he simply won't let us play to any kind of audience till he's sure the play is as good as we can get it."

Finally, the Monday before the Thursday opening, Oliver broke down and announced that everybody who belonged to the Playhouse, plus whatever visiting theater people turned up, would be allowed to see that night's practice performance. He gave them such short notice that Ginny didn't have time to work up her stage fright.

Selena was out there, in a short evening dress, trailing a gray mink cape, because she was going to a party afterward. John Pauling, the business manager, was there, and a handful of those unknown men sitting with Gordon Tyler, all of them looking worried.

Altogether, the audience consisted only of about 50 people. Ginny didn't know all this until afterward, and she wasn't scared. As Bill had told her to do, she did her best.

It seemed to her that things went very well. There was quite a lot of clapping after the first two acts, though with so few people, the clapping sounded hollow. There was clapping after the last act too. Yet, when they came off Amanda did not look cheerful. "Is anything wrong, do you think?" Ginny asked with a tight throat. "Did they like it?"

Amanda recovered her smile and touched Ginny's cheek. "Never, *never* ask that," she warned. "It's the real audience, Thursday night, that we have to worry about."

Ginny nodded and tried to smile. But when she was home in bed she couldn't get to sleep at all until the sky started to grow light. After all, Amanda had *not* answered her question.

After that night, Ginny felt as though she had suddenly been pushed from behind by a force she couldn't even name, much less control. Faster and faster it moved her, and up at the top, hidden in a black cloud, was a door marked Opening Night. What would happen when it opened? Would it lead out into something like a little-girl view of fairyland? Or would she step through it into . . . nothing?

She had been counting days. After Tuesday, she began counting the hours. Before she knew where she was, they were down to twelve, then six, then four. Her father wanted to leave the store to drive her to the theater.

"That's silly, Dad. I can go on the bus, as I always do. You would only have to come back and have dinner and make the trip all over again to get yourself and Mother to the Playhouse again."

"The whole trip's only about 20 minutes," Mr. Harris pointed out. Ginny won. She couldn't have explained it, but she had to go on the bus. She just had to do everything as if it were any ordinary day.

Just as she went through the stage door, which since Monday had been manned by a plump, cheerful old fellow named Ben, Ginny was seized with a terrible fit of shivering.

"It's a chill! I've caught some horrible disease!" she thought in fright. "I won't be able to go on!"

CHAPTER 11

The Kindest Way

Ginny didn't know how long afterward it was that she was sitting in her dressing room, back to the mirror, drinking something that burned her throat out of a tiny silver cup. "Better?" Oliver asked, taking the cup.

Ginny swallowed to see if the burning had done permanent damage, but it hadn't. "What happened? I didn't faint, did I? I never fainted in my life!"

"This would be the time to start, then," Oliver said. "No, you didn't faint, you simply stood there like something out of a church yard on Halloween. I never saw anything quite like it. Ben dragged you back here and came for me. Are you all right now?"

"How can anyone be all right tonight?" Ginny asked in fear. "Oh, Oliver, do you think—"

"None of that!" Oliver said quickly. "Nobody thinks tonight. We just get on with the job. When you are all pulled together, come around and have a sandwich. We are all having a prisoner's last meal in my office."

Oliver's office was banked with flowers like a funeral parlor, and though there were enough people in it to make a party, it felt more like a wake. Only David and Toni were really eating. There was a little talk, but nobody laughed. The few bites of chicken sandwich Ginny forced down stuck in her throat.

It was still early, so Toni and Ginny walked around to see how the Playhouse was going to look to the paying customers.

It was surprising how different it was. Before, it had seemed, most of the time, like an empty house. Now, suddenly, it had come alive. John Pauling and Gary, who had come back from New York that morning, were in the ticket booth; the front doors were spread open and the newly painted entrance hall, with its crystal lights, seemed to promise even better things beyond. Toni held Ginny's hand.

"Time to start dressing," she said. Then she paused. "I want to say something. I was hurt when Oliver gave you that part. It's true that you are exactly right for it, and I'm all wrong. And I knew he had to do this particular play for a lot of reasons, but I felt I had a right to the first young-girl part, and I—well, I'm just mean."

She leaned forward and gave Ginny's cheek a smacking

kiss. "I know you felt it and I want to say right now I only care about your going in there and knocking their eyes out. You do it, you hear me?" She gave Ginny a little shake and pulled her around to the side door. There was no more time. This was it.

Inside, everything had changed, too. There was a kind of buzz running through the whole place. While Ginny got into her costume, two phone calls came in for her. Toni took both messages—one from Madeline, one from Emmy. There was a constant going and coming in the passage as telegrams were delivered.

There were telegrams for Ginny from Miss Cameron, two of her aunts, several Margetson people and one from, of all people, Cappy Roberts! "'Good luck to the only famous person I know so far,'" Toni read. "Who's Cappy Roberts? Ginny stop that laughing!"

Ginny, the eye pencil shaking in her hand, tried to stop. But it was so funny! Cappy Roberts had always been such an important person to her, had seemed to have all the wonderful things—friends and quick wit. And here he was, sending *her* a telegram because she was opening in a real, live play!

In quick succession, Amanda and David came in to kiss Ginny. Oliver stopped in, and Clay and Miss Harper. Nobody said "good luck." That, Toni had explained, was the worst wish you could make. At one point, Toni closed herself out into the passage and then came back in, looking upset. "Your mother was out there, but I told her it was against the rules, so she just said to kiss you for her."

Then, suddenly, Bill was in the room and Ginny was in his arms, her calm and control completely forgotten.

"How did you get in here?" Ginny asked. "When did you come?"

Bill laughed. "Did you think I wouldn't be here? Didn't my flowers come, and my note?"

"Oliver's got a thing about flowers. He has them all stuck in his office till the performance is over," Toni fluttered. "I will go see—"

Ginny seized Bill's hands. "Bill, I must have been crazy! I can't go out there—"

Bill rocked her back and forth. "Of course you can. You've done all the work. All you have to do now is go out and show it."

There was another knock at the door and the call, "Fifteen minutes, Ginny." Then the door was blown open as if by a strong wind, and Selena swept in. She glared at Bill. Hastily, Ginny introduced him. Selena took her hands off her hips, looked him up and down. "Very nice," she said. "But, get out. I want to help this child make up her face."

Ginny, blushing, was proud that Bill smiled as though movie stars told him every day that he was "very nice." He gave Ginny a quick kiss on the cheek, a squeeze of the hand, and then went out.

Things became very wild. Selena fussed and pulled and poked, and every few minutes the voice outside made the time shorter. And all at once the call came, "Time, Ginny."

From long practice, Ginny's feet hurried her to the right place. The set—the old kitchen—had been up for several days. Behind it, a fake wall hid the combination wire, wood and cheese cloth which lighting magic would turn into the "hill" for Ginny to climb.

Toni touched her shoulder and showed her where to peek out into the audience, and Ginny's heart pounded madly when she saw that the small theater was jammed. She had never realized before what a beautiful little place it was. She crossed her fingers and breathed hard as the lights went down. They *had* to like it. It *had* to be good.

This was only the third time in her life that Ginny Harris played to a real audience. But as she went through her part, she knew something was wrong. "They are not with us," she thought once. "They don't believe us."

She knew it as certainly as if they had stood up and shouted it out. There was absolute silence; there was no coughing or movement out there to bother the actors. Yet Ginny knew—and though David and Amanda were putting their hearts into their performances, she sensed that they knew it, too.

At the end of the first act, they all went straight to their dressing rooms without speaking. Gary and Toni had been told to hang around near the entrance, listening to people's comments. When Toni came back just before Act Two, she wore a bright wooden smile and announced that everyone was saying it was terribly *interesting*.

Act Two ended with a movement of excitement: disturbed by the lover's strange effect on her mother, Bonnie snatched up a knife and threatened him. The curtain came down to a lot more clapping than before. Feeling better, Ginny heard David say to Oliver back stage, "When the second act is good, you've got them."

Oliver answered, "Not true, like all those old saws." Ginny didn't know what to think. Peeking into Amanda's dressing room through the half-open door, she saw that Amanda was quietly knitting. But Amanda was always knitting.

Somewhere in the middle of the third act, Ginny knew. It was very simple. She was so conscious of the audience that her mind wasn't really on the play at all. And if she wasn't lost in it, they couldn't be. By the time she made her final exit, going slowly up the hill and over the top, down the ladder on the hidden side, she knew that *Top of the Hill*—in theater talk—had laid an egg.

Nobody said it, back stage, afterward, in all the noise and buzzing talk. Her own dressing room was packed. It was really a party, and when you had a party you were celebrating.

Ginny had her first taste of wine and began to think that perhaps she had been wrong—after all, what did she know? But as the visitors were clearing out to let the actors dress, she heard a snatch of talk between Oliver and John Pauling. John asked if Oliver was going to wait up for the papers, and Oliver answered no, he thought that morning would be time enough.

"Whoever wants to is invited to come over to the Brockford House Coffee Shop for a while," Oliver added. "Might as well cheer each other up." John spread the word around, and everybody in the company went, except Ginny. All Ginny wanted was to climb into her bed and pull the covers up over her head.

But it wasn't until morning that Ginny learned how really bad things were. She woke up with sadness weighing her down. That feeling of something gone wrong . . . and Oliver not wanting to wait up for the papers. The papers! Wildly, Ginny jumped out of bed, pulled on her slippers and robe and almost fell down the stairs. Her mother and father stopped talking as she shot into the kitchen.

"Go back to bed, dear. You deserve a nice long rest," Mrs. Harris said. There was a fat pile of newspapers on the counter, and Mr. Harris was trying to fold down the one he held and hide it somehow under his coffee cup.

Mr. Harris said in anger, "I'd like to go down and punch old Ed Williams in the nose. Who does he think he is, with his small-town newspaper?"

But it wasn't the local paper, or the *Brockford Signal* that hit Ginny the hardest. They had tried to give the Playhouse the benefit of the doubt. Both reviews praised the beauty of the new theater and welcomed it as a "wonderful addition to the local scene." They didn't get to the actual play until down near the end. The local *Sentinel* said much the same thing in better language. It added, "Amanda Massey and David Wainsford gave professional performances in this interesting play, but they did not have much to work with. Ginette Harris, the young Glenside actress who is making her professional start with the Playhouse, was the third member of the cast."

But the New York papers . . . ! "*Top of the Hill* belongs at the bottom of the class," said the *Times*. "This stiff little item is false to the bone. Amanda Massey and David Wainsford turn in their usual fine jobs, and Oliver Williams will certainly do interesting things in the future, but he will have to find better plays."

The *Tribune* was as bad. In other words, but just as chilling, it said that the play had been terrible. And as far as both the *Times* and the *Tribune* knew, there might have been no living human being named Ginette Harris. They simply did not mention her at all—as though that were the kindest way.

CHAPTER 12

Ginny Makes a Decision

Ginny realized later that she must have been in a state of shock. But at the time it seemed to her that she was taking things quite well. She couldn't share her father's great rage against the newspapers. If the play was bad, they had to say so, didn't they? It was the job of the man who reviewed the play to say what he thought. And if Ginny Harris was a flop, it was better for them not to mention her, wasn't it?

It wasn't until she got back upstairs that she began to hurt. "Ginny Harris . . . that's me," she thought. "Of *course* I'm a rotten actress! Of course I have no talent! I kept telling them!" She put her head in her hands, trying to squeeze back the tears. She had told them all! From Mr. Feld, with his crazy notion that she ought to join the Drama Club, right down the line—or up—to Oliver Williams.

All morning the phone kept ringing, but Ginny wouldn't talk to anyone, not even Bill. She was getting dressed to go over to Brockford, and she was thinking. By the time she was ready, she knew exactly what she had to do.

It was a nice, sunny day, and the Playhouse had a business-as-usual air that surprised Ginny. Peering inside, she saw the stage crew moving out the last few *Top of the Hill* props. Oliver must have decided to make the first performance the last.

Nobody else was around. But as she approached the office, Ginny heard voices. The door opened and Toni came out. She looked angry, and her eyes were bright as though tears lay behind them. "Hi," she said without much spirit. "How come you aren't home sleeping it off like everyone else?"

"Sleeping. How can anyone sleep after the papers—"

"Well, I don't mean *sleeping*," Toni said. "But you know—taking it easy and getting ready for whatever comes next. Actually, Amanda's gone in to New York to do something or other about her apartment there, and David's out shopping for some new clothes. How are you feeling, by the way?"

Ginny shook her head in a helpless way. She was crushed, bleeding, broken—and Amanda and David had gone cheerfully about doing common, ordinary things.

"I won't be long," she told Toni. "Can you wait for me? We could have coffee or something . . ." She was really thinking, *We can say good-by,* but she didn't want to tell anyone until she told Oliver himself.

"Well, Ginny," Oliver said, looking up with a smile from his desk. "I hope you are weathering the storm— I mean the reviews and all that."

Ginny bit her lip. "I don't want to think about that, Oliver. I only came to say—that I'm as sorry as I can be for letting everyone down, and of course I'm leaving the company."

"Of course *what?*" Oliver came around to lean against the desk with folded arms and stare down at her. "When you've just started? Look here—our next play simply must be some good old sure-fire thing with a part in it for Selena, because her name will pull them in and we've got to make up, fast, what we've lost. But I've got the most marvelous thing in mind to follow. It's got magnificent parts for both you and Toni. Take home a copy of the play—"

"Oliver, please!" Ginny cried. "Please don't be so kind! If it hadn't been for me, you might have had a success last night." She put her hands over her face.

"My dear girl, you are a nut," Oliver said calmly. "*Top of the Hill* was simply my mistake, that's all. It would have had a hard time going over on Broadway, where people at least are used to the kind of thing it was trying to do. Out here, where nobody has seen much theater of any kind, quite frankly I must have been out of my head to try it. But there's not much lost as long as we wrap it up and get to something that can't miss."

"But you read the reviews! If I had been any good at all—"

Oliver snapped his fingers. "Look, Ginny, trust me—I've been in this business a thousand years. Toni was just in here begging me to give her a chance at the Bonnie part. Toni's good; do you think I wouldn't keep the play going and let her have a shot at the part if I thought for a minute it would make any difference? It wasn't you, Ginny, I promise you! The play was wrong from every angle—wrong for us, wrong for the town!"

Ginny stood up. "It doesn't matter," she said. "I could never go out on a stage again." Her voice began to tremble. "Thank you for everything, Oliver," she managed to add, and ran out.

Later, as she and Toni sat over coffee at a drug store near Toni's Y, Toni said suddenly, "I'm quitting too." She nodded at Ginny's surprise. "Yes I just made up my mind. Oliver's not going to give me a real chance. I will just hang around doing the dirty work—"

"But you can't quit, Toni! You've never wanted to do anything but act! It's different with me—I was on the wrong track from the beginning."

Toni shook her head. "No more than I was. Who cares that I've wanted to act? It doesn't count unless you prove you can do it. I haven't proved it yet, and I'm darned

if I'm going to get fat and lose my looks while I'm waiting around for a chance to prove it. No—I'm going back
to New York and work in a dress shop a friend of mine
owns."

Ginny tried a few more arguments, but she couldn't
argue very hard against something she was going to do
herself.

"My friend has been after me for years to work for
her, and now I'm going to," Toni declared. "I can get
to love clothes as much as I thought I loved the theater.
And, at least, if you sell a woman a dress that makes
her look beautiful, everyone can see what you've done!"

"And I will go back to Margetson's," Ginny said. "If
I ever get to New York, and if I have enough money,
I will come and buy something from you, Toni."

"Special prices for friends," Toni grinned. The girls
got down from their stools and stood for a minute. Ginny
held out her hand. Then, quickly, she leaned forward and
kissed Toni on the cheek, and Toni hugged her. Ginny
felt as though she were saying good-by to someone she
had known very well for a long time.

Ginny went first to Margetson's, where she had already
made an appointment with Mrs. Winters. She had
known somehow that it would be simpler to face her
parents with all her bridges burned, and a job at Margetson's waiting for her. Later, she would have to explain
to Bill, face-to-face.

Ginny spent the rest of the day writing notes to David,

Amanda and the others at the Playhouse to say good-by, and bracing herself for the announcement to her parents. She knew her father would try to argue her out of it, and that her mother would cry.

It all happened just as she expected. Her father lost his temper at her "foolish" idea, her mother cried and even tried to call Madeline to come and talk Ginny out of it, but by great good fortune Madeline's number didn't answer.

Then, little by little, Ginny began to feel better. Maybe the Playhouse hadn't been such a bad experience after all. Maybe it had given her at least some of the confidence in herself she had been so very sadly lacking before!

She had a chance to test this before she expected it. On Monday, when she reported to Mrs. Winters, she was greeted with a small bomb shell. "How would you like to try selling, instead of working in the office?" Mrs. Winters asked.

Selling—out on the floor, turning a bright, helpful smile on one person after another, making conversation with strangers? Ginny stared at Mrs. Winters. Somehow, the more she thought about how awful it would be, the more interested she became.

She heard herself say, "I would love to, Mrs. Winters—" and immediately started to take the words back, but it was too late. Before she could stop the wheels, Ginny found herself on the main floor of the biggest department store in town—feeling both good and bad.

She was supposed to move around to fill in wherever extra help was needed. For the first day, Ginny went around with a "Buddy," a tall girl named Marge Hale, who told her where to look for things and how to write up sales checks, and which sales girls to watch for tips on handling customers.

After that, Ginny was more or less on her own. The first few times she asked a customer "Can I help you?" she was afraid the woman would hear her knees knocking together. Then suddenly, she wasn't scared at all! When Bill phoned to ask how it was going, she told him proudly, "I go right up to them, Bill! No problems!"

"Wait till the first time one of them bites you," Bill said. "You won't talk so big!"

"I'm loving it," Ginny said firmly. It was almost true. As she explained to Bill, she felt as though she had had lots of experience selling. She even encouraged him to hang around for a few minutes on the main floor while she took care of a customer so he could see with his own eyes that she was doing it well. He announced that he was so pleased with her sales manner that he would treat her to dinner at the Lake Lodge.

Ginny's eyes opened wide. The Lake Lodge was so expensive that she had never been there, and didn't know many people who had.

"Hang the expense," Bill said grandly. "We're celebrating your new career and my new raise—small though it is!"

Later, when they were settled at a table looking out over Glenside Lake, and the waiter had gone with their order, Bill looked at Ginny thoughtfully. "To go back to all that talk about celebrating, Ginny—are you sure that's how you feel about your selling job?"

Ginny nodded. "I like it, Bill, I really do. I've been thinking a lot about it. I've decided that the whole business with the Playhouse, and trying to be an actress, had a purpose in it. At first I kept telling myself what a fool I had been to even think of a stage career, and that I deserved what I got. But—well, you know how I was before. I could never have gone up to a customer and offered to sell her something. I wouldn't have known what to say! Now—I like it. So the whole experience was good for me."

Bill still looked as though he had his doubts. "You mean that all the excitement and challenge of the Playhouse didn't mean as much to you as a job selling hats at Margetson's? It's like exchanging the moon for a toy balloon, Ginny!"

"You work at Margetson's! And you seem to be satisfied!"

"Ginny, that's different." Bill shook his head, his brown eyes serious. "I've never wanted to do anything but run a store—the bigger the better, sure, but that will come someday. Meanwhile, I even like what I'm doing. But when a man like Oliver Williams tells you you can act—that *is* the moon, Ginny, compared with what you are doing."

Ginny was afraid they were on the edge of a quarrel. Her heart was pounding. "Maybe I don't want the moon," she said. "Can't you believe that? Some people aren't meant to reach out for impossible things. I just want to feel that I could get along with other people in the ordinary world—the way I never used to be able to. Now I'm beginning to do it. That's *all* I want, Bill!"

Bill reached over and covered her hand. "All right. But do you remember the famous line from some play or other we had to read in school—*Methinks the lady doth protest too much?* Stop trying so hard to make me believe you, and then maybe I will," he said.

They didn't come that close to fighting again. After a while, even Ginny's parents stopped giving her sad looks. They seemed to accept the fact that they were not, after all, going to have a famous daughter. The weeks of fall went by and Ginny began to feel that she was really quite content. She was doing well. Mrs. Winters, reviewing her record, told her that most of the head people in the departments where she had worked had asked for her as a permanent member of their crews.

But Ginny hoped a permanent place could be put off. She was happier moving around, selling something different every few days. The truth was, she got a little bored when it was one purse after another, or one sweater after another.

One afternoon, as she was handing over a customer's wrapped package, somebody behind her said, "How about a ham sandwich, Ginny?" She wheeled around, saw an attractive young man in an Air Force uniform, and exclaimed, "Mike Dyne!"

Mike grinned down at her. "Who else is always trying to force a sandwich on you? Gosh, Ginny, you look wonderful! How are you? Have you seen . . ." For a few minutes they tossed names back and forth, filling each other in on the friends who had scattered in June.

Mike was home now for a ten-day leave. He had come to the store to buy his mother a birthday present. Ginny led him to the jewelry counter, where she was working.

"Your mother would love this bracelet," she told him firmly.

Laughing, Mike bought it, but when she gave him his change he seemed in no hurry to go.

"Somebody I ran into told me you got interested in the stage, Ginny," he said. "I guess after that crazy mixed-up business with the Drama Club—remember? How would you like to go over to this new Playhouse in Brockford with me tomorrow night?"

Ginny flushed. She didn't want to go to see Amanda and Selena and the others in *Private Lives*, which was what the Playhouse was putting on now. "I'm sorry," she told Mike a bit shyly. "But I—well, I—"

"Going steady, I guess," Mike finished. Ginny nodded. "Ah, well, I guess I got the message the day you turned down my sandwich. Best of luck, Ginny!" With a wave and a grin he was gone, leaving Ginny staring after him with mixed feelings. Mike Dyne . . . he might have been interested in her, back at school? He had thought she was cool to *him?*

Would wonders never cease? "And not only that," Ginny thought as she went back to work, "not only that! There I was, chattering away to Mike Dyne as though we had once been bosom buddies, saying more to him in ten minutes than in four years of school . . . Why," Ginny told herself, smiling in a foolish way at a puzzled lady who immediately took off the hat she was trying on—"I've graduated! I'm just like real people now!"

It was a few days later that Mrs. Winters asked Ginny to stop at her office. She was nervous as she stood before Mrs. Winters. It never took much for her old doubts to come creeping back into her bones . . . never as bad as the old days, to be sure, but always ready to make her heart pound and her throat go tight. Still, Mrs. Winters was smiling. Ginny tried to smile back.

"Ginny, I have an early Christmas present for you," Mrs. Winters said. Glancing at her calendar, she added, "Six weeks early, but still it's not going to happen until after Christmas, so—how would you like to be junior assistant in Miss Patton's department?"

Ginny stared. "It's a promotion," she told herself. "Don't just stand here. Say something. Say thank you!"

But her heart had sunk right down into her shoes.

CHAPTER 13

Reaching for the Moon

Junior Assistant! This was not just another job. Everyone knew it was an important step up the ladder at Margetson's. Mrs. Winters had every right to sit waiting, with a pleased expression, for Ginny's thanks.

"I don't know what to s-say," Ginny told her. "Miss Patton doesn't even know my name."

"She doesn't, actually," Mrs. Winters replied. "But you did such a nice job when you worked for her that she asked for you."

Ginny said slowly, "I wouldn't be selling."

"You would be behind the scenes, learning how the office runs. It doesn't pay any more than you are making, to start," Mrs. Winters warned.

But it wasn't the money. It was something more. What

it was, Ginny couldn't be sure. Why would a girl who had just been given a nice promotion feel as if something dreadful had happened?

But strangely, Bill wasn't much help that evening. "You must not want the new job," he remarked.

"How could I not want it?" Ginny frowned. "Whatever it is that bothers me, I wish I could figure it out, and forget it. If I don't show more interest, Mrs. Winters may decide on someone else for the job."

Bill drove along in silence for a while. "How would you feel if that happened?"

"Awful! Of course I want the job! It's a real, serious job—like yours, Bill—not just standing around handling nice things and talking to people."

In bed that night, Ginny sat for a long time in her thinking position, arms around her knees and her chin resting on them. The truth was, she would be relieved if someone else got the job.

Why did she want to go on selling, she wondered. Was it because selling was kind of like being on the stage, really? With each customer, didn't you ask yourself, *What kind of person will it take to convince her that she needs that blouse?* "At least that's the way I do it," Ginny thought. "Why, I'm putting on an act as a sales girl! I act a dozen different ones each day!"

Ginny swung herself off the bed and padded down to the bathroom for a glass of water. She decided to take a pill too. By the ache that was beginning somewhere around her heart, she knew that she was getting near the truth, and she didn't want to lie awake all night while it crept in on her.

She didn't want to start thinking about the bare stage of the Playhouse the day she had read for Oliver, or about the cold cream-and-dust smell of the dressing rooms, or about David and Amanda and the others. Most of all, she wouldn't let herself think about the feeling she had when the house lights went down and the only real world was the one that she and the other actors created.

The next day, Ginny decided to put aside all such thoughts. She kept telling herself firmly, "It's all settled. I'm going to take this job and do the best I can with it. It's exactly the kind of work I should be doing. It's right for me."

And then, suddenly, she caught sight of a familiar slim figure on the other side of a rack of wool slacks.

"Toni!" Ginny exclaimed, then flushed as everyone within range turned around. The girl turned too. It *was* Toni. Her smile flashed as Ginny hurried around the rack and grabbed her hands.

"Can you talk here?" Toni demanded. "I came in on purpose to look for you—I just stopped at these slacks because they are so nice and cheap. Oh, Ginny, it's so good to see you!"

Ginny glanced around. Miss Salcott, the assistant in the department, was watching her with raised eyebrows. Quickly Ginny snatched four pairs of slacks from the rack. "Follow me, please," she said, leading Toni to the dressing rooms.

"I will even buy a pair so as not to make a liar out of you," Toni said, holding bright green slacks up against herself. "Here—these will fit. Now tell me all about everything. Do you like it here?"

Ginny told Toni everything in very few words. It was Toni she wanted to hear about—Toni, who was supposed to be working in a dress shop in New York.

Toni looked guilty. "Well—it's like this, Ginny," she said. "I tried working with Nina, and it was fun for a while. I guess I'd still be there if—oh, well." She flushed. "Oliver whistled for me and I came running, that's all. He rang me up three days ago to say he was making up the cast for their next play and there was a part he'd like to see me in. I practically flew."

"Well, that's wonderful," Ginny said over the sudden catch in her throat.

"When I think of all those speeches we made to each other about being through with the theater—" Toni gave Ginny a keen look. "How about you, Ginny?"

Ginny busied herself hanging up the slacks Toni was not going to buy, and went out to put them back on the rack and pick up her sales book. When she got back she was able to say quite calmly, "I never think about it, Toni. After all, I wasn't ever really part of the theater the way the rest of you were. I found out pretty fast."

"Oliver doesn't agree. He asked about you practically

the first thing. Wanted to know if I thought you would be interested in reading for a part." Ginny bent over her sales book to hide the excitement she knew must have flashed across her face.

"Do you know what Oliver told me?" Toni went on. "He said you were scared off too easily. He said you had plenty of talent, but you didn't belong in the theater if you could be discouraged so easily."

Toni looked directly at Ginny. "You have to have drive. You have to want this kind of work enough to fight through all the bad reviews and learn from all the mistakes to make yourself better. Maybe it was too easy for you before. Everyone pushed you and urged you. If you want to work in the theater enough to come back and ask for a second chance—well, maybe that will be the real beginning for you."

Toni finished, "I know you could get this part— Ginny, please, *please* think about it."

"Yes, and then have everyone ask what makes this girl think she's an actress? And perhaps even spoil the whole play the way I did the last time." Ginny's hands shook as she finished writing out the sales check. "I won't try again, Toni. I was never meant to try to do wonderful things or to—to reach for the moon. I like working here!" She would have looked more as though she meant it if tears hadn't started to run down her cheeks.

Miss Salcott's voice came coldly through the dressing-room passage. "Ginny? If you are free, one of your customers is waiting." Hastily, Ginny mopped her eyes. She had no special customers—that was Miss Salcott's way of telling her that she was spending too much time in the dressing room with Toni.

"Here's my phone number, Ginny," Toni said quickly. "Will you call me so we can get together?"

Ginny promised. Seeing Toni had been wonderful. Of course she would see Toni again. Maybe she and Bill could even go to see the new play. By that time, surely she would be able to walk into the Playhouse without all these mixed-up feelings.

Ginny went home from work that night with a headache that sent her straight upstairs to her room. She stretched out on her bed.

"Who am I kidding?" Ginny suddenly asked herself aloud. She sat up and put her hand to her forehead. This was a *problem* headache, the kind she used to get before examinations. It meant there was something bothering her—something she hadn't been able to figure out.

"And I know what it is, too," she went on. "I'd better stop trying to tell myself I don't."

She heard the sound of her father's car and then the door downstairs, which meant her parents were home. Quickly she went into the bathroom and washed, and brushed her hair.

Bill called her as they were sitting down to dinner. "How are you?" he asked as though somehow he knew.

"I'm fine," Ginny assured him. "Everything's all right."

Then she caught sight of herself in the hall mirror and slowly shook her head. "That's a lie, Bill," she said. "I'm all up in the air. Bill—would you drive me over to Brockford tonight?"

"Sure," Bill said. "What for?"

"To the Playhouse, of course!" Ginny tried to be patient. After all, was there anything else in Brockford she wanted to see?

"You mean you want to see the show they're putting on?" Bill asked. "I thought you wanted to stay away from the place."

"I did, Bill. I still do—I mean I don't want to see the play. I just want to go over and—look." Ginny couldn't explain what she meant. But somehow she knew it was the right thing to do. She would go over and look at the Playhouse, face-to-face. Then maybe she would know, once and for all.

They didn't talk much on the way over. Just before they got there, Bill warned, "It's theater time, Ginny. It will be all lit up, with people going in . . ."

"I know. Don't worry, Bill. It won't make me unhappy. Not that way, I mean. I have to see it."

Bill nodded. "All right, I won't ask questions. When you are ready to talk, just start talking." He drove one more block, swung around a corner, and there was the Playhouse. It shone in its frame of lights. The parking lot was jammed. People were going in between the framed posters that announced, "Oliver Williams' pro-

duction of *Private Lives,* starring Selena Bryce. . . ."

Bill pulled into a space opposite the entrance, and they watched while people who were late jumped out of taxis and hurried inside. Ginny wondered who was taking tickets. She wondered if Toni was lending a hand back stage or if the Playhouse was now doing so well that they had all sorts of people for the odd jobs. She sat with her arms folded on the rolled-down window and watched until long after the curtain must have gone up. Finally she raised her head.

"I guess I'm going to try after all, Bill," she said happily. "I'm going to try for the moon."

"If you mean what I think you mean, I'm glad, Ginny!" Bill took her hand. "I've had a feeling all along that you really wanted to go back to the theater."

Ginny shook her head. "I really had myself convinced that all I wanted was a quiet job at Margetson's. But I've really been on stage the whole time. I've been playing the part of a sales girl—of a lot of different sales girls."

She laughed at Bill's expression. "I've been doing a lot of thinking since Mrs. Winters told me about my new job. There had to be some reason why the new job made me so miserable. And it's really very simple. I realized I'd have to stop playing different parts and I—well, I didn't want to stop."

"Everybody who's worth anything has to try for what he wants," Bill said seriously. "Haven't you always known that? I have. With me it's simple! I'm doing what I want to do already. But whatever it is, however hard, even if you think it might be impossible, you have to take a stab at it, Ginny!"

Ginny nodded. Tomorrow she would call Oliver and ask if she could read for the part in the new play. Just thinking about getting out on the stage again, speaking words that made a person come alive even though she didn't exist—just remembering made Ginny hot and cold.

She looked up at the sky. Only stars up there tonight —no moon. Yet Ginny saw a moon—the one she was going to reach for . . . not shyly, afraid to try too hard, but this time with all her might.

She might not make it. But to reach for it was better than to curl up in a corner with her hands over her eyes, pretending she didn't care. And maybe, Ginny thought —maybe if she tried hard enough, she could at least get a few miles closer to it . . . close enough for the glow of it to light up her life.

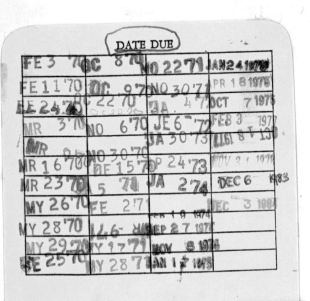

F   **Fiore, Evelyn**
Fio   Ginny Harris on stage

POTTERVILLE MIDDLE SCHOOL